CHOCOLATE-BOX HEARTS

JOSIE RIVIERA

5 STAR READER REVIEWS

Amazon Review by B (A Chocolate-Box Christmas)

"Oh what a great start to a new series. It's an easy , short story to read and perfect for this time of year . Maise is a food journalist and is judging a chocolate contest. Every girls dream job, right? Not true for Maise, but she is determined to get through it. Ben is an interesting contestant and you'll have to read the story to find out more about how things go.

Entertaining, sweet, heartwarming moments drew me in from the very first page. Now, I'm looking forward to the next book in the series."

Amazon Review by Marie B. (A Chocolate-Box New Years)

"This story had me at fresh homemade pasta. Julie is right and the dry kind just doesn't compare. I don't have it very often, but I love it when the restaurant I'm eating at offers it. Julie and Lorenzo had a whirlwind romance with misunderstandings, which started when she thought he was married and hitting on her. I loved reading about all the wonderful food she made. I've never had cassata, but is sounds yummy. I liked that they bonded over their love of film noir, something else that I've never truly experienced. There were plenty of funny, romantic, and sweet moments in this clean holiday food filled romance."

Amazon Review by Mary F. (A Chocolate-Box Valentine)

"A Chocolate-Box Valentine is a sweet addition to author Josie Riviera's chocolate-box series.

In this novella, chocolate plays a role in the romance – but probably not in quite the way you might expect.

Keep in mind that this is a novella, so things move along a lot faster than you would expect in real life. Even within the confines of this short book, the author is still able to bring her characters to life. I loved the way she was able to bring an immediate connection between Sally and Oliver because they both owned food establishments. A fallen tree serves as the perfect mechanism to provide a reason for them to spend time together.

Extend your Valentine's Day by an hour or two and curl up someplace comfy and cozy to read this delightful story."

INTRODUCTION

To keep up on newly released ebooks, paperbacks, Large Print Paperbacks, audiobooks, as well as exclusive sales, sign up for Josie's Newsletter today.

As a thank you, I'll send you a Free PDF ... The Beauty Of ...

Josie's Newsletter

Did you know that according to a Yale University study, people who read books live longer?

This book is dedicated to all my wonderful readers who have supported me every inch of the way.
THANK YOU!

CONTENTS

PRAISE AND AWARDS

DEAR FRIENDS

Dear Friends,

A heartwarming story is the hallmark of a romantic read. Savor the magic of the holidays with this collection of three clean and wholesome romances.

Find out why readers are falling in love with **Chocolate-Box Hearts** & staying up all night reading! These romances will warm your heart.

Cozy up with your favorite beverage, and lose yourself in the joyful seasons of love.

A Chocolate-Box Christmas

This short and sweet romance is a #1 Amazon Bestseller.

Love is sweeter with a touch of mischief.

Judging a chocolate-making competition for the women's shelter's annual fundraiser should be an easy, even pleasurable, assignment for Maise, new food critic for the *Bloomingfield Daily Dispatch*. Too bad just the smell of chocolate makes her stomach roil.

By the time she reaches the last table, she hopes her face

isn't as green as her holiday sweater. But the tall, square-jawed man behind piles of fudge makes her want to linger, even savor the moment along with his chocolate-coffee-flavored confection.

Except there's something Ben Elliot is hiding behind his piercing blue eyes and lazy grin, and her reporter's nose senses a story worth exploring. She finds herself longing to discover the secret ingredient sweetening their mutual attraction.

A Chocolate-Box New Years

This holiday story is a top 100 Amazon bestseller in clean and wholesome, as well as holiday fiction romance.

Some recipes don't turn out quite as you predicted…

The extra time and expense of Julie Elliot's old-school cooking methods are worth it, but that means The Pasta Junction's bottom line is often stretched thin—much like herself. Even during the holidays, the restaurant's busiest season.

When she carves out time in her brutal schedule to meet with Bloomingfield weatherman Lorenzo Rossi, she crushes her reaction to the tall, blue-eyed charmer quicker and harder than a clove of roasted garlic. Lorenzo may be sweet as Italian cassata and hot as a red pepper, but *planning an anniversary dinner* means *married,* and she needs another disaster like that like she needs another olive oil stain on her shirt.

But as she and Lorenzo assemble the ingredients for a perfect celebration, she discovers something completely unexpected. And her heart may not withstand the storm of emotion she never saw coming.

A Chocolate-Box Valentine

A short and sweet romance for a quick, quick read.

It's your last love who truly matters.

Owning a candy store should be a fun and delightful profession. Besides, what candy could beat Sally Elliot's signature coffee chocolate fudge?

None, except for the unique infusion candy she designed for Valentine's Day.

Unfortunately, the signature chocolate required for the candy won't be delivered on time.

No problem. She'll pick up the order herself.

When she reaches the diner where the delivery man is stranded, she retrieves the chocolate and intends to return to her shop. But a downed tree detains her. And the handsome, kind man who owns the diner makes her want to stay, especially after she accepts his challenge to prepare homemade delectable chocolates with him.

There's something about Oliver Menroe's gentle mannerisms, his genuine interest in his customers, that ignites a hope Sally had extinguished long ago. As a disillusioned single mother, she knows from experience that love doesn't last forever.

But can she allow herself to believe that one simple ingredient can sweeten their mutual attraction and … for the first time in her life … create a lasting love?

JOSIE RIVIERA

a Chocolate-Box Christmas

PRAISE AND AWARDS

CHAPTER ONE

*M*aise Anderson stood at the entrance to the women's shelter in her new hometown, her gaze fastened on the front door. The weather was a typical mid-December afternoon in California, but she was accustomed to cooler temperatures.

However, this wasn't about winter. This was about chocolate.

Under normal circumstances, she would have admired the magnificent landscape surrounding the town of Bloomingfield —the imposing snow-capped mountains, the towering ponderosa pines—but she couldn't, because all she focused on was reaching for the metal door handle and turning it.

With a nervous inhale, she gave herself a stern reminder.

You can accomplish this simple assignment. Candy is a sweet holiday treat. Besides, everyone loves chocolate.

Maybe. Maybe not.

She hadn't eaten chocolate in over two years because of a nasty bout of food poisoning.

Nonetheless, she hadn't gotten sick because of the chocolate, she rationalized, as she recalled that particular dining assignment. Most likely, she'd gotten sick because of her entrée.

She flicked a glance toward the leaden sky, grimacing when a brisk wind blew misty rain across her face. A chill rose up her neck and she shivered.

She tucked her small umbrella under her arm and pressed her lips together.

Outwardly, she passed for the ideal food critic. Her shoulder-length chestnut hair was pulled into a classic chignon, her beige leather pumps sported a sensible heel, and her camel-colored blazer was tasteful and practical. She'd opted for tailored navy-blue slacks, topped with an emerald-green turtleneck sweater, holiday looking but conservative. She'd kept her makeup to a minimum—muted red lipstick, a light rosy blush, and mascara to highlight her green eyes.

Confidence and expertise on the outside. Foreboding and anxiety on the inside.

She blew out a whoosh of air, straightened her shoulders, and pushed open the door to the shelter. "Here we go," she said under her breath. "I can withstand anything for an hour."

"Happy holidays, Miss Anderson." The mayor, Ed Johnson, a thin man but with a wide grin to make up for it, hailed her as she stepped inside. They'd met at a Hometown Holiday event at the County Museum the previous weekend. "There's a cold front coming in. I'm pleased you agreed to judge our annual fund-raiser."

"I'm happy to participate," she lied. In reality, she had no choice. Her boss, the editor of *Bloomingfield Daily Dispatch*, had given her the assignment with a gruff, "There's no food budget for this affair. Take a couple of pictures with your phone camera, sample the weirdest piece of chocolate you can find, and follow up with a full-of-praise article."

Such was the job of a food-writer reporter. No extravagant feast or fancy sushi. Just pure, sweet chocolate.

At the thought, her stomach roiled.

"Are you settling into your role as our town's newest food critic?" Ed asked.

"Yes." She tempered her voice to sound calm and professional. "There's a wealth of fine restaurants here."

"You're originally from Anchorage, Alaska, correct?" He accepted her blazer as she shrugged it off, hanging it on a coat rack and placing her umbrella beneath it. "California's weather must feel quite warm compared to the frozen north."

"Anchorage winters are certainly memorable." She smiled, well remembering the freezing temperatures and shortened daytime hours that descended on the city from September to May.

"My wife saved your piece in the newspaper about preparing a week's worth of meals ahead of time. She prefers to eat out, but she actually cooked and froze five dinners." Ed reached for a piece of peanut butter fudge on a side table and popped it into his mouth.

"I'm glad my article was helpful." Maise followed him into the dining hall. Eight tables were set up, each covered with a red velvet tablecloth and laden with silver-plated chocolate displays. The entrants, men and women of all ages, stood behind their respective tables and eyed the mayor, then Maise, nervously.

An undecorated Scotch pine soared in the corner of the large room. Beneath the tree, gaily wrapped packages donated by the community were earmarked for the children. The previous day, Ed explained, the shelter had held a Christmas caroling party. Today, most of the women were out job hunting while their children attended school.

Though Maise tried to maintain a semblance of composure, the scents of sweet and bittersweet chocolate filled the air, and she choked back the nausea in her throat.

"Smell that?" Ed inhaled deeply and smacked his lips.

"Peppermint fudge, my favorite. This fund-raiser is a choco-holic's dream."

Or nightmare.

She extended a gamely smile, sending a stern command to her queasy stomach to settle.

"All the candies are handmade from the local shops and restaurants," Ed continued. "From my experience, all women love chocolate, so you must have jumped at this assignment."

Jumped? Umm, no. Actually, she'd cringed.

But she couldn't refuse. She'd been on the job less than a month and had finally settled into her comfortable second-floor apartment at the edge of town. She had no intention of moving back to Alaska and hoped to make Bloomingfield her permanent home.

In Anchorage, her five older brothers had doted on her, while she'd been suffocated by controlling parents who constantly argued. She'd moved away, much to her brothers' dismay, but she wanted to prove to herself that she could manage her life independently.

"Well, I didn't really jump," she said.

"Watching the waistline, right? If I was paid to eat out, I'd gain a pound a week."

She fumbled to say more, but he'd turned to welcome the two other judges. The man and woman, who appeared to be in their early sixties, regarded Maise with smug superiority.

Maise understood that she was in a competitive business, and the unspoken truth that came with it. In food journalism, as in most professions, it was necessary to prove oneself in order to establish a distinguished reputation.

A cheerful rendition of "Rudolph the Red-Nosed Rein-deer," sung by Gene Autry, played on repeat, and Ed sang along for a few measures. She grinned as he enhanced his singing with a little dance.

When the song began another loop, Ed led the judges to the tables.

"Here are the eight hopeful candymakers." He exchanged a grin with the woman behind the first table, then motioned to an adjacent counter. "Judges, if you want water or coffee in between bites, it's here."

Coffee. Her favorite beverage. Maise regarded the steaming foam cups set on the counter and whispered an appreciative thank you.

As they went down the line of tables, Ed presented the judges to the candymakers, and Maise realized that she already knew two entrants from her recent assignments. Both were restaurateurs, and both acknowledged her. But the other six entrants were strangers. As she tried to remember all the names Ed recited, she paused at the last table. A tall, lean man with a strong, square jawline and solemn demeanor was being introduced.

He was startlingly handsome, with piercing blue eyes and dark curly hair.

"This serious guy is Ben Elliot." Ed surveyed Ben's table, the glass apothecary jars bursting with peanut butter brittle, and the red bento boxes labeled Bean-to-Bar Chocolate. "Everything looks good, Ben."

"Thanks." Ben gave a quiet sigh and tossed aside a cardboard bento box he'd been trying to put together.

The mayor and judges started back to the first table, but Maise lingered. "Aren't you happy you're here, Mr. Elliot?" she asked. "You don't look as thrilled as the other candymakers."

"Like you, I couldn't be more delighted to be here." He met her gaze, and a lazy smile swept across his face. He'd obviously been watching her and had noticed her apprehensive scan of the displays.

She pulled a notepad and pen from her tote bag and

flashed him a polite smile. "And what exactly is bean-to-bar chocolate?"

"Why? Is this an interrogation?"

She frowned. "Isn't this a chocolate contest? I'm a judge and—"

"I don't believe the contest has started yet." He glanced at his watch. "Would you like to try a chocolate-covered almond while you wait?"

"No. No, thank you." She angled away from him. She knew her complexion had gone pale at the mention of chocolate. Nevertheless, his admiring stare roved over her face, then glided down her body to her feet, which were shifting restlessly.

"And your name is—" he inquired.

"Maise Anderson. The mayor just introduced me."

"Right." His lips quirked. "You're a bit nervous this afternoon, Miss Anderson. Brand-new on the job, I take it? I read your recent critique in the newspaper about The Pasta Junction, an established restaurant in town. Apparently you don't like pasta?"

"Pasta is my favorite food."

"Really? You certainly didn't mince words in the article. What were some phrases you used ...? Oh yes, the sun-dried tomatoes were too dry, and the pasta stuck together."

She stiffened. "I give my honest opinion, without malice. Most restaurants want feedback so that they can get better."

"You recommended that The Pasta Junction add pizza to their menu."

"Because they serve Italian cuisine, I assumed pizza might be offered, perhaps for lunch, if not for dinner."

"I can assure you that pizza hasn't been added. My sister, Julie, owns that restaurant." He regarded Maise in impassive silence. "If she wanted to sell pizza, she'd open a corner pizzeria, not an upscale Italian restaurant that's been in business for ten years."

Maise kept her posture strong, although inwardly her chest felt like it was caving in. She truly wanted diners to discover new restaurants because of her articles. "I realize the word 'critic' may have a negative connotation, but I write honestly and fairly."

"Let's not forget that it's all through your perspective and therefore colored by your opinion. It's up to the reader whether to agree or disagree with you."

Curtly, she nodded. "Correct." She kept her gaze steady and her chin high. Her self-assurance came partly because he'd laced his voice with a teasing tone, and partly because of his good-natured grin.

"Mr. Elliot, please tell your sister that the antipasto was delicious and I look forward to visiting her restaurant again."

"Ben."

She tipped her head. "Excuse me?"

"My name is Ben. May I call you by your first name, Maise?"

"Of course. There's no need for formality." She met his stare. "Rest assured, Ben, I strive to judge restaurants impartially. Surely you must realize my critiques can't be all fluff."

"An impartial food judge." Mayor Ed had returned and gazed at her with a gratified grin. "You're exactly what our little town needs to put it on the map. I read about your writing expertise in Anchorage, a city five times the size of Bloomingfield. Your stellar review of The Moose's Pad helped launch that restaurant. Diners wouldn't have discovered it otherwise."

She winced, remembering the nasty emails she'd received. "Not everyone agreed with my review."

"Apparently enough people did. Your article was picked up by several major newspapers."

Which had been the problem. In a big city, she'd been expected to write ten to twenty posts a week, plus restaurant reviews, plus handle the social media that came with it. After her article exploded, the workload had doubled.

A thoughtful, well-reported piece took time, and she'd begun to burn out. A small town like Bloomingfield was just what she needed to decompress. She'd still do what she loved, but at a slower pace.

Nevertheless, Ed was a skillful politician, strategically spinning the conversation in order to praise her, and the realization made Maise grin.

Ben grinned at the same time, and they shared a chuckle. Belatedly realizing that he might be flirting with her, she took a guarded step backward. He stood only a few feet away, casually dressed in dark pants and a white polo shirt, and became far more handsome the longer she stared at him. His blue eyes were bringing unexpected changes to her heartbeat.

And there it was. An unanticipated magnetism. An attraction that drew her wholly by surprise.

Mayor Ed tossed a piece of peppermint fudge into his mouth and chewed while he spoke. "Ben Elliot is the owner of Bloomingfield Candy Shop."

"All that?" Maise looked directly at Ben.

"All that and more," Ben quipped, then met the mayor's gaze. "Correction, Ed. I'm the co-owner."

"The man behind the scenes. Don't let his unassuming manner fool you, Maise. This guy is our very own small-town hero."

Why, she wanted to ask, but Ed was ushering her back to the coffee table, where the other judges waited.

He addressed the three of them. "Folks, the directions are simple. Sample the candies and write down your thoughts and criticisms. You can visit the tables in whichever order you choose. Give the candy a score between one and ten—ten being the most delicious." He eyed the sturdy wooden clock hung on a bare wall. "It's two o'clock, everyone is here and we'll begin. By three o'clock, you should be finished. Bring your comments and scores to me. Ready?"

"Ready!" Maise forced an upbeat tone and made her way to the first table while the other judges dispersed.

"This is a pepper truffle," the wiry ginger-haired candy-maker said, quickly enlightening her. He handed her a piece set on a red lace napkin. "Try it."

"You mean a *peppermint* truffle?"

He gave her a knowing look and didn't reply.

She took a deep breath and sampled a bite. Immediately, her eyes watered. She'd expected something sweet with a cooling aftertaste. This candy wasn't sweet. It was flaming hot.

"No, I mean pepper," the man replied. "It's made with red pepper flakes and a dash of pepper oil. A light tang to chocolate candy gives it a punch, wouldn't you agree? It packs a hint of unexpected spicy heat."

Jerkily, Maise bobbed her head, although she wanted to point out that the heat level was more than a hint. While he went on to describe the process of tempering chocolate, she grabbed some water from the counter and greedily drank. Then she switched to a cup of black coffee and sipped appreciatively.

"I worked in France as an assistant chocolatier before opening my own shop," he said. "No doubt a person like you is aware that candy making requires a special skill."

She nodded as she jotted notes on her notepad. "Anything else?"

"Don't get water in the chocolate while you're heating it, because the process will be ruined."

"Thank you." Her stomach rebelled, and she eyed the

other seven tables. She snapped a picture and stepped unsteadily to table number two.

She hoped the dark lemon crème candy, charmingly showcased on a linen napkin, might soothe her stomach. It didn't. Maise thanked the chocolatier, took a quick picture, and moved on.

At table three, a blond woman presented Maise with a piece of white chocolate shaped like a candy bar.

"What are the red specks?" Maise asked.

"Strawberries and rose petals, and the petals are edible," the woman replied. "Taste it."

Maise inhaled, then nibbled. "Delicious," she assured. The woman didn't seem to notice Maise's shudder while she explained the difference between pure white chocolate and dark chocolate.

"Did you know that white chocolate is simply cocoa butter and sugar?" the woman quizzed.

"I know now." Maise thanked her, then swiveled to the counter, pondering if she should grab another cup of coffee. The caffeine rush seemed to help her to carry on.

She did, and it helped again.

That is, until she tried the candy at the next four tables.

It was a struggle, and she knew that the fixed, objective expression on her face was slowly disintegrating.

By the time she neared Ben's table, she only had one thought. How could she get out of there? Wildly, her gaze searched for the exit, and she peered at the clock on the wall.

Only a few more minutes. Would it really matter if she skipped his table? He probably wouldn't even notice.

She started toward Mayor Ed, intending to leave. She'd hand in her notes and give Ben's chocolate a score of ...

"Hello, Miss Maise. Or is it Mrs.?" Ben called out to her.

Her lips parted, and she spun to regard him.

That was his greeting? *That* was his question?

She squinted against the sickness in her throat and treated his remark with dull courtesy. "I'm not married."

She'd been engaged when she lived in Alaska, but had decided to break it off. Now, in her early thirties, love didn't come easy for her. Perhaps because she was commitment shy after her argumentative parents had finally divorced once Maise and her brothers had gone off to college.

"Good." He lifted a dark eyebrow. "Were you going somewhere and trying to skip me?"

She stepped to his table, heat flooding her face. "No, I ... Well, yes." She sighed. "It's been a long day." She braced herself for his reprimand.

Instead, he offered a simple, tender smile. "Sorry. I've watched you since you walked in, and I wanted to chat."

So he had been watching her. Her cheeks warmed, and a thrill of excitement heightened her senses as he openly admired her.

"Then you have more than one intrusive question?" she asked.

Her reproof brought a smile to his lips. "Many more."

"May I ask a question too?"

"About me? Sure. I'm an open book."

"Are you married?"

"Divorced. Two years ago," he said quietly. "And a bachelor at thirty-five."

She hung back. *So he was single too.*

"I'm glad you're here," he went on. "Our town prides itself on its good taste." Ben laughed at his pun and Maise's heart did a surprising leap. He threw her totally off-balance, and the composure she'd desperately tried to maintain tumbled a notch.

"I was thrilled by the newspaper's generous job offer," she said.

"All this opportunity in one small California town." Again,

she was taken aback by his fine features. His thick hair was a tad too long, those deep-set eyes a vivid blue, and he sported the physique of a well-toned athlete.

Maise stalled and took a sip of her coffee. "Will you explain your candy-making process, Ben?"

He shuffled his feet. "What would you like to know?"

"All the other contestants expounded on their delicious candy. I assumed you would do the same."

"I don't want to oversell my product."

"I find that remarkably refreshing and humble." With laughing relentlessness, she continued, "But I'm still interested."

"Would you like a piece of our shop's signature chocolate coffee fudge?" His gaze drifted to her lips, then to the cup she'd set on the corner of the table. His deep tone had a persuasive gentle quality. "I've noticed that you like coffee. Isn't that your second cup?"

"My third, if you count this morning." She pulled her gaze from his and stared at the cup, anything to delay eating another bite of candy.

She took another sip of coffee, and the most surprising thing happened. Here, amidst all this chocolate, her nausea seemed to dissipate, and she began to relax.

Was it the coffee? Or the man standing a few feet away, his gaze riveted on her?

Shakily, she chuckled. "I'll jot down your comments." Noting that his head drooped ever-so-slightly, she asked, "That is, if it's okay?"

"Of course." He avoided eye contact, or maybe she was imagining it.

"Good." She poised her pen on the notepad. "Can you begin by explaining your candy-making process?"

. . .

*B*en felt his muscles tense. He wanted to answer her, but he couldn't follow through if her questions became too exacting.

"For instance," she was saying, "what are the exact ingredients in your signature chocolate coffee fudge?"

"Let me think about it." He swallowed hard, trying to remember what Gee, an excellent employee who had given his sister the recipe, had told him numerous times.

"Still thinking?" Maise prodded after a lengthy beat. Her enchanting features, a clear, porcelain complexion with a smattering of freckles, a pert, upturned nose, and her full pink lips holding a hint of a smile, made him hesitate.

Was she on to him?

Absolutely not. How could she be? They'd only just met.

He glanced at her profile as she scribbled on the notepad —the profile he'd admired ever since she entered the room. Her tall, slender figure was model-like, and her huge green eyes—enhanced by full black lashes and a touch of mischief— were magnificent.

A touch of mischief.

"What are you writing?" he asked, finally breaking the silence. "I haven't said anything."

"I'm writing my grocery list."

Her reply made him laugh.

"I'm still waiting," she reminded, pen poised on the notepad.

He wet his lips and combed through his mind for any details that might be helpful. "Well, our secret ingredient is ... coffee."

"In coffee fudge, I wouldn't call coffee a secret ingredient."

"And marshmallows," he hastened to assure her. Gee had mentioned marshmallows in the recipe, hadn't she?

"Chocolate too, I suppose?"

"Yes, yes, of course." Ignoring Maise's furrowed eyebrows, he placed a chunk of fudge on a white lacy napkin and presented it to her. "The final test is in the tasting, don't you agree?"

She lowered her gaze and muttered something that sounded like, "I'm finally beginning to feel better, and I can't eat another piece of chocolate."

But she didn't look sick.

He reached across the table and lightly touched her arm. "The candy from Bloomingfield Candy Shop is the best. I genuinely believe that to be true."

"Which is through your perspective and therefore colored by your opinion?" She echoed his earlier remark. "Please clarify so that my readers will understand."

"Because our ... chocolate chips are ... sweet."

Her face glowed with laughter. "You mean semisweet?"

He squirmed. "Yes, yes, that's it." With an apologetic grin, he lifted the candy toward her. "Take a bite."

There was something about her over-bright smile that made him suspicious.

"You don't like chocolate, do you?"

A rosy blush stole up her cheeks, and she bent her head, shoving a wayward strand of thick chestnut hair behind her ear.

"You don't like chocolate?" he repeated. Desperately, he struggled to keep his features straight.

"Not today."

He crossed his arms. "A food critic judging a chocolate candy event who doesn't like chocolate."

"I said not today."

"What about tomorrow?"

She fumbled with her bag, her movements both graceful and endearingly awkward. "Two years ago, I had a bout of food poisoning after eating stinkhead and then topped the meal with chocolate for dessert. The memory stuck with me."

"What on earth is stinkhead?"

"It's the mushy fermented head of a king salmon and a delicacy in Alaska. I wrote a review of my experience in the Anchorage newspaper, minus the food-poisoning incident."

Despite her professional tone, her voice quivered. He had the uneasy feeling that he had somehow hit a nerve.

"So, the article wasn't a success?"

"That's putting it mildly." She bit on her lower lip and looked down at her hands.

"Look, I'm sorry about what I said earlier. Your review of my sister's restaurant has actually brought in more diners."

"Apology accepted." Slowly, the embarrassment drained from Maise's face.

Across the room, Mayor Ed was conversing with the other judges.

"Enough about me." Maise plunked her hands on her slim hips. "Let's have a heart-to-heart about you, Mr. Chocolatier. Admit that you have no idea what you're talking about."

"You discovered my secret." He chuckled with relief. "What I know about chocolate could fit into a peanut butter cup. I'm just the businessman who owns the shop. My sister, Sally, makes all the candy. I'm covering for her today, as her daughter is home sick. She's a single parent."

"So you have two sisters? Julie owns The Pasta Junction, and Sally runs Bloomingfield Candy Shop?"

"And a third, Katie, who is a lawyer." Ruefully, he shrugged. "I'm besieged by females."

Maise laughed. "In Alaska, I was surrounded by five brothers."

"So why did you leave?"

"Many reasons. You listened to one of them."

"I'd like to hear the others." Because he wanted to get to know her better.

"I started to lose my readership and credibility," she replied, "after patrons complained that a restaurant I wrote a glowing review for served sub-par food."

He heard the disheartened tone in her voice. "Don't take it to heart." He smiled as Gene Autry began singing again about knowing Dasher and Dancer and Prancer and Vixen.

"This song has been in the same loop at least nineteen times."

"Twenty by my count," Maise said.

"Are you feeling any better? Will you try a taste of my shop's signature chocolate?"

Hesitantly, she accepted his offering, then closed her eyes as she took a bite. Her eyes popped open. "Ben, this is delicious."

"It's my favorite."

"Mmm. I forgot how much I love the combination of coffee and chocolate."

"So, Bloomingfield Candy Shop gets a perfect score?"

"Are you trying to sway me? I'm the judge, you're the contestant." She wrote a number on her notepad, then leaned over the table and whispered, "Is there any way I can make a clean getaway?"

He nodded toward the exit and gave a cheerful wave to Ed, who eyed them warily.

"Thanks." Maise snatched another piece of coffee chocolate fudge, then stepped toward Ed. She handed him her notes, grabbed her blazer and umbrella, and studiously avoided Ben's gaze as she departed.

Still, he laughed when he saw that she'd finished his chocolate.

CHAPTER TWO

*C*hristmas Eve came a week later. As usual, Maise hadn't completed her shopping, because buying for five adult brothers and her parents was more than difficult.

It was impossible.

She parked her Volkswagen at the curb of Main Street and stepped out of the car, smoothing her red-and white-striped dress. California weather was mild, almost balmy, and she loved it.

She peered around. Hopefully, a few shops were open, and she'd know the right gift when she came upon it.

A sign in the window of Bloomingfield Candy Shop caught her attention.

Winner of the Women's Shelter Annual Fund-raiser for best candy. Come in for a free taste of flavor-rich fudge.

The shop's red canopied entrance welcomed her as she entered, and she admired the tin pails and decorative boxes tied with exquisite satin bows. The scents of high-quality handmade chocolates combined with the aromas of butter, vanilla, and sugar. Truly, this shop was a chocolate lovers dream.

She'd pondered her conversation with Ben that day at the shelter. At first, she'd thought he was just schmoozing her to win her vote. But no, he'd been sincere. And besides, his candy had deserved to win.

"Maise!" A handsome, familiar man behind the counter greeted her as she stood at the end of a long line. When it was her turn, he quickly filled her order for seven boxes of chocolate.

"Do you ship to Alaska?" she asked.

"We ship all over the world."

"Can you put a rush on it? It's for my five brothers and my divorced parents who live separately."

"Chocolate is sent two-day air, so it won't be overexposed to the elements. However, your family won't receive the candy in time for Christmas."

"I always run behind. I'll call them on Christmas Day and explain."

Ben added a complimentary cup of hot chocolate and an extra box of signature fudge to her order and placed them on the counter.

"I'll help you drink the hot chocolate," he replied as she raised her eyebrows. "I wasn't supposed to be here tonight, but wanted to lend a hand because of the last-minute rush. My sister left a few minutes ago to be with her child. You just missed her."

"It's Christmas Eve and completely understandable."

He gazed at her for a long moment. Around them, the shop began closing down, and he bid his employees a joyful holiday.

He raised the cup of hot chocolate to her. "Merry Christmas, Maise."

"Merry Christmas, Ben."

"What are you doing this evening?"

"I'm attending a church service at the little chapel in town, then will order a pizza and going home."

"I'll accompany you." His infectious smile made her immediately agree. "But I planned to make a stop at a military service family's home. I'm a volunteer for the USO."

"Is that part of your small-town hero story?"

He nodded.

"I'm fascinated." She swallowed a sip of hot chocolate, then put the cup aside on the counter. "What do you do for the USO?"

"Anything and everything. I'm dedicated to our service members. But mostly, I provide a listening ear."

"Can I visit them with you?"

"I'd like that very much." He took an easy breath and placed her candy in a bag. "Afterward, we can dine at a distinguished Italian restaurant."

"And what's the name of this distinguished restaurant?"

"The Pasta Junction." He caught her hand and led her out the door. "My sister's restaurant stays open late on Christmas Eve."

Maise grinned. "Does she offer pizza?"

"Nope. But I have it on excellent authority that she serves a delicious antipasto."

HE END

A NOTE FROM JOSIE

Dear Friends,

Thank you for reading *A Chocolate-Box Christmas*.

I wanted to write a short, sweet holiday story centering around chocolate.

Please help other people find *A Chocolate-Box Christmas* by posting your review.

A Chocolate-Box Christmas is available in ebook, paperback, audiobook, and Large Print paperback.

I'd love to meet you in person someday, but in the meantime, all I can offer is a sincere and grateful thank you. Without your support, my books would not be possible.

As I write my next sweet or inspirational romance, remember this: Have you ever tried something you were afraid to try because it mattered so much to you? I did, when I started writing. Take the chance, and just do something you love.

Happy Holidays!

My Spotify Play List for A Chocolate-Box Christmas is here.

With sincere appreciation,
Josie Riviera

Love sweet romance holiday stories?
   Be sure to check out my holiday book bundles:
   Holiday Hearts Volume One
   Holiday Hearts Volume Two
   Holiday Hearts Book Bundle Volume Three
   Holiday Hearts Volume Four

Want the individual books of the Chocolate-Box Series?
Click here.

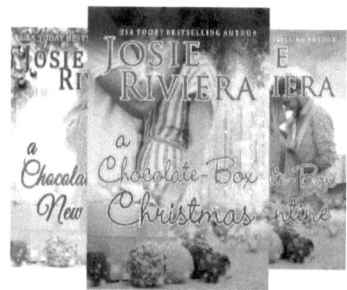

RECIPE FOR CHOCOLATE COFFEE FUDGE

From Gee's Kitchen

Ingredients

    ¼ cup freeze dried coffee granules (Can use decaf)
    2/3 cup canned evaporated milk
    ½ cup (1 stick) butter
    2 ounces baking bar chocolate – broken
    1 ½ cups white granulated sugar
    2 cups mini marshmallows
    1 cup real chocolate chips (semisweet)
    ½ teaspoon vanilla extract

Prepare a rectangle cake pan lined with parchment paper or aluminum foil with enough overhang that you can lift fudge out for cutting. For thicker fudge use an 8 inch x 8 inch pan.

Large pot (or use a wok)

Place milk and coffee in pot over medium heat, stirring to dissolve the coffee.

Now add the butter, sugar, and baking chocolate with the pot on medium high heat and stir occasionally while they melt adding the marshmallows next. Bring contents to a boil and boil for 5 minutes stirring constantly.

Remove the pot from the heat and add the chocolate chips stirring to dissolve. Add the vanilla extract (it will bubble) stirring till glossy.

Pour into prepared pan and smooth top. Let set on a flat surface for an hour and then refrigerate.

Remove from refrigerator, lift up paper/foil and place on a cutting board. Cut into squares.

Store in an airtight container.

Don't forget to sample the crumbs.

Josie Riviera

a Chocolate-Box New Years

This book is dedicated to all my wonderful readers who have supported me every inch of the way.
THANK YOU!

PRAISE AND AWARDS

USA TODAY bestselling author

Top 100 Amazon Bestseller Clean and Wholesome Romance (Books)

Top 100 Amazon Bestseller Holiday Fiction (Books)

CHAPTER ONE

*I*n the intricate process of making fresh pasta, the
dough has to be kneaded, rolled, and then sliced.
Every morning Julie Elliot made the flour and egg base,
portioned it, and stored it in her cooler. In this way, she could
quickly create satisfying meals for her customers, which was
of utmost importance in the restaurant business.

Consequently, it made sense that her linguine and fettuccini were the starring attractions of her Italian restaurant,
The Pasta Junction. She liked that, being celebrated for her
delectable pasta versus the parboil method other restaurants
used.

As expected, many rival chefs told her she was foolish, because preparing pasta every day required a tremendous amount of effort. She realized that and was okay with it. She'd set her standards high and strove to serve her diners only the finest products.

On a typical busy Friday evening in mid-December, she stood by the commercial cooktop of her kitchen's workstation and stirred an enormous pot of minestrone soup. When she finished, she'd chat with patrons in the dining room. She loved people, loved interacting with them. Loved it so much, in fact, her older brother, Ben, often called her an extrovert. As a business owner, that was a good thing. Striking up conversations and conversing with her customers kept them coming back.

Because she didn't stay in the kitchen all night, she made sure she looked attractive and professional. Tonight, she'd pulled her heavy blond tresses into a tight bun, and wore her usual black slacks and a fitted collared blouse. As always, she'd tied a white apron around her slender waist.

She lowered the fire under the soup so it would simmer, then swung to the stainless steel counter to sort green beans. After a few minutes of discarding the beans that weren't fresh, she paused to scan the other workstations. In an adjacent corner a newbie created salads. Nearby, a grill cook prepared chicken dishes. He held his tongs and grill brushes high, flicking dashes of red pepper and sea salt onto the sizzling chicken.

Her gaze traveled to Antonio, the sous chef, who stood across from her. His bald head was covered by a pleated white toque hat—starched, round, and ten inches high—and a white coat. Antonio subscribed to a kitchen hierarchy and believed the head chef should wear the tallest hat, and he took his job very seriously. As she observed him, he flash-fried shrimp in garlic butter, tossing the mixture with a flamboyance rivaling any celebrity chef.

With a tolerant smile, she began snapping the stems off the beans.

Certainly homemade pasta, homemade anything, really, was twice the effort, and her employees often struggled to keep up with orders on fast-paced nights. But it was worth it.

With a sigh, she blew a wisp of hair off her forehead.

Or was it?

Earlier in the evening, a part-time employee had quit with no notice, and Julie had asked—okay, begged—a member of her prep team to put in a double shift. Not long afterward, a server spilled olive oil on a woman's silk dress, a cook burned his fingers on a steamer, and a waiter tripped over a loose wire in the foyer, dropping an armload of ceramic dishes that had crashed to the floor and shattered into hundreds of pieces.

A glance at her watch prompted her to wryly shake her head. Quite an eventful evening, considering it was only seven o'clock. Already exhausted with an impending headache, she scraped up an armful of beans, intending to rinse them in cold water to remove any dust and dirt.

The phone buzzed, and Julie frowned. No one in the front of the house called the back unless there was a problem.

She set down the beans, snapped off her sanitary gloves, and answered the phone. "Yes?"

"A guy on line three insists on speaking with you," the hostess said.

"We're in the middle of the dinner hour and swamped with orders."

"It's Lorenzo Rossi."

"The meteorologist from the six o'clock news? Why? Is he forecasting another thunderstorm?" Julie asked. "Two weeks ago he panicked the entire community when he raised an alarm about a dangerous storm with potential flood warning, and his forecast was incorrect. We closed early, and the storm bypassed our area."

"Give him credit. He gets the weather right some of the time." The hostess giggled, which was odd. Usually, she was proper and polite, but Julie attributed the giggling to the fact that Lorenzo Rossi was drop-dead gorgeous.

"Shall I tell him to phone back after we close at ten?" the hostess suggested.

Rapidly, Julie considered her options.

Perhaps he was calling to promote her restaurant on TV? After The Pasta Junction's recent less-than-stellar review by the new food critic in Bloomingfield, the positive endorsement from Lorenzo might be a bonus.

"Put him through," Julie said.

"Anything you say, boss."

Julie grinned and accepted the call.

"Julie Elliot?" Lorenzo's voice was deep and familiar, sounding exactly like the man she watched at the end of the day on the television station's website. Instantly, her mind conjured up his handsome face, the black wavy hair and his vivid blue eyes. Similar to his fellow newsmen who wore sport coats and dress pants, Lorenzo clicked it up a notch and wore classic, three-piece suits. And his tone—strong and masculine, with a slight Italian accent.

Julie cupped the phone to her ear. "Yes, this is she."

"My name is Lorenzo Rossi."

"What can I do for you, Mr. Rossi?"

"I'm calling about New Year's Day. Your restaurant is one of the few places in town that are open."

"Christmas and New Years are special occasions. I'm happy to give families and friends the opportunity to dine out together." Plus, the decision to remain open on those holidays had proved profitable. "We'd love to have you join us here at The Pasta Junction. I'll switch you back to the hostess to make a reservation."

"I'd like to book a first-wedding-anniversary dinner."

"The front desk will confirm the number of people in your party."

"Also, I want to serve a special dessert, my grandma Gloria's Italian Cassata."

"My pastry chef can accommodate you." Although the chef had recently quit too, and the restaurant had begun outsourcing their desserts. She didn't have the heart to tell Mr. Rossi that bit of news. She didn't have the heart to tell herself it would cost $2000 to train a new chef.

"Do you know what a cassata is?"

Julie bristled. "A cassata is an Italian cheesecake."

"You're recognized for making genuine homemade pasta."

"Correct."

"Because of your commitment to authenticity, I expect you'll be able to replicate my grandmother's cassata recipe."

"Can you supply us with the recipe, Mr. Rossi?"

"Gladly." Silence prevailed for a beat. "I remember her cheesecake overflowed with chocolate. May I set up an appointment to discuss it?"

He requested an appointment to discuss a cheesecake?

She stared at the phone. "Certainly."

"Excellent," he said. "People rave about your professionalism."

"That's our motto. Professionalism."

Now why had she professed such a thing? Professionalism wasn't the motto, although it was a goal she tried hard to achieve.

However, he could easily reserve online, and email her the recipe. She told him as much, giving him the restaurant's website.

"I've checked it, but I'd still like to meet with you."

Julie's gaze wandered to Antonio as he chopped garlic for another shrimp dinner. An overabundance of garlic would overpower the meal, she thought. Frazzled, she cradled the phone and took a step forward to stop him.

"Miss Elliot?"

Julie nodded into the phone, a silly gesture because Mr. Rossi couldn't see it. "Yes?"

"Will tomorrow morning be agreeable? I need to be at the television studio by noon."

"Mornings are best for me too." *And he apparently wasn't giving her any choice.* Still, she prided herself on excellent customer service and quickly agreed. He expected professionalism, and she would comply.

"Nine o'clock?" he asked.

"Sure. I'll show you several catering menus, and you can choose which meal will suit your party best."

"Thank you, Miss Elliot." He hesitated. "I assume it's Miss—"

"It is." She'd never married, never really dated, except the one occasion when she'd fallen hard for a guy who'd made it a habit to dine alone at her restaurant. He'd flirted with her, and at first she'd enjoyed the attention. Then she'd found out he was married and studiously ignored him until he'd gotten the hint and not come around anymore.

A two-timer. A cheater. No thank you.

Nowadays she was wed to her work, anyway. She kept the barrier shielding her heart intact and secure. Getting involved with a man had proven to be a bad idea.

"Please call me Julie, Mr. Rossi," she said.

"Thank you, Julie, and Mr. Rossi is too formal. I'm Lorenzo."

"See you in the morning, Lorenzo. Remember to bring your grandmother's recipe."

After assuring that he would, he thanked her and hung up.

For a minute she was quiet, ignoring the chattering cooks and hurried footsteps as they scurried through the wide kitchen.

So the gorgeous Lorenzo Rossi was celebrating his first wedding anniversary? As far as she knew, he'd never revealed anything about his personal life on television, but then, why would he? To her knowledge, his marriage hadn't been announced in the local newspaper, either.

Naturally, his career was forecasting the weather, oftentimes focusing on catastrophic events. California's severe storms and the ever-present threat of wildfires had lately made headline news.

But there were times when his forecasts were lighthearted. She recalled one particular forecast when the temperatures on his weather map were in the negatives—minus 50 degrees Fahrenheit in Anaheim, minus 75 in Los Angeles. Lorenzo had kept his cool, (literally), smiling and pointing out the temperatures with a quip.

"Folks, you may wish to bundle up if you're traveling to these cities today, as well as bring an extra stockpile of gloves. I wouldn't plan on getting my car washed in either place, and I'm anticipating school will be canceled." He'd laughed. "Or better yet, just wait until the spring thaw."

He'd thought quickly and on his feet during the live broadcast. He evidently had a sense of humor.

Grinning with the remembrance, she scooped up the beans and carried them to the sink.

There must be a reasonable explanation why Lorenzo Rossi requested a meeting in person, rather than an online reservation. Surely, this wasn't because of a cheesecake recipe.

Either way, a wonderful surprise was in store for the undoubtedly stunning Mrs. Rossi. Lorenzo was apparently a thoughtful husband who planned ahead, intending to create a perfect anniversary for his wife.

Julie smiled. The wedded bliss of newlyweds was a fanciful prospect. Too bad falling in love was something she never intended to do again. The sting of a disastrous relationship was too great a price to bear.

CHAPTER TWO

The following morning, Julie entered The Pasta Junction an hour later than she'd intended. She'd scheduled an interview for a new hire at eight and then planned to review vast amounts of paperwork with her manager before Lorenzo arrived.

Because of her lateness, she'd canceled both the interview and the paperwork review. The previous evening's disasters had required her to remain at the restaurant until well past midnight.

When her alarm woke her at half past seven, she'd hastily showered, dressed in her customary black blouse and slacks, then tugged on a pair of skid-resistant work shoes. Around her neck she tied an emerald-green silk scarf, flicking the lace edging over her shoulder. She styled her hair in pin curls and finger waves, dusted translucent powder on her face, then added dark mascara and red lipstick.

She rushed through the rain into the restaurant, shaking the raindrops from her slick yellow jacket and signature black fedora. She hung both on a coat rack. She'd don the fedora later that evening when she chatted with guests.

Tonight she intended to devote only a few minutes to the kitchen. Large crowds energized her, and reservations were at a max. This was typical for a Saturday, and since this was the holiday season, people were on vacation and eating out more often with family and friends.

She stepped through the silent dining room and quickly arranged pink roses in bud vases, placing one at each table. She'd kept the festive décor to a tasteful minimum—fragrant evergreens draped on the fireplace mantel, and tiny colored lights along the stairwell. She'd preserved an old world Italian atmosphere, complete with classic white tablecloths and huge murals of Italy's countryside. Scenic Tuscany vineyards exuded true European charm.

The Pasta Junction had had several name changes throughout its half century and recently had been declared a Bloomingfield historic landmark.

At this hour, the space was quiet. The servers had set up the tables the night before for the luncheon crowd, and the doors would open at eleven o'clock.

She ducked into the kitchen and brewed a pot of coffee, noting the burrs had begun to dull, a reminder the commercial coffee grinder needed repair.

Money was tight, though. Despite the extra traffic, the additional staffing during the holidays came with a price tag.

As she did every morning, she went through the leftover pasta and made a mental note to donate it to the local charity.

Delicious food, particularly pasta, was an obsession of hers, and through the years she'd perfected her craft. Nothing beat the thrill of her customers' compliments and return visits, the smiles on their faces when they experienced the light, delicate flavor of her specialty fettuccini. She was passionate about her work and enjoyed adding new dishes.

Sometimes she started with a recipe, sometimes only an idea, and followed her instincts as often as any written directions.

Nonetheless, a continuous loss of product and thus, revenue, was a growing concern. She had costed out the ingredients and knew she was financially ahead by making her own pasta. However, a waitress had told her that several patrons had walked out the evening before because of the over-long wait. That had been happening too much lately, and Julie rebuked herself. She'd been too busy and was ignoring her staff's feedback.

She began boxing the leftover pasta, trying to understand why she was so driven. Pasta making was not only time-consuming, it was a risky venture. Her updated waste log pinpointed the main revenue problem was the pasta, along with her sous chef over-ordering fresh garlic, which often went bad. And come January, when business slowed, she frequently faced difficulty meeting payroll.

But for the month of December, profits were excellent.

With a satisfied sigh, she dismissed her reservations and plucked a marinated shrimp from the reach-in cooler. A whiff of garlic pinched her nostrils. Just as she feared, the sous chef was overpowering the food with garlic. As she placed the shrimp on a plate to sample later, a glob of congealed butter landed on her blouse.

"Oh, no," she muttered. Rushing to the sink, she snatched a clean towel and moistened it with water. A hard scrub on the grease mark soon left a prominent wet stain. She fanned the stain, trying to recall if she had a spare blouse at the restaurant, or if she had the time to go home and change before lunch.

The doorbell jingled, and she peered at her watch.

Lorenzo? Already? She washed her hands, hastened to the foyer and opened the door.

It was indeed him, standing on the steps, prompting her heart to do an unexpected flip.

Why this strange reaction? She was familiar with his appearance. But in person? Well, that was another story entirely.

He was easily over six feet tall, slim, and wonderfully fit. She'd heard television added pounds to a person's frame. In his case, he looked exactly the same.

"Julie?" He snapped his umbrella closed, then removed his eyeglasses and tucked them into the pocket of his worn leather jacket.

"Yes. Hello, Lorenzo. Please come in." He was early, but she wasn't going to hold that against him, a wet spot on her blouse or not. She admired punctuality, although she was seriously lacking in that department. She rationalized it was because she tried to do too much by herself and refused to delegate.

"Thank you." He stepped into the flagstone-tiled foyer and looked around, his gaze settling on the chalkboard where she wrote the day's specialties. Fettuccini was always on the board, as were the two entrees from the previous night: a creamy risotto and veal flank steak with red-hot peppers.

He considered the restaurant's interior. Then his gaze rested on Julie's face. "Nice." He beamed his approval. He didn't seem to notice the conspicuous stain.

She flushed.

"Everything exceeds my expectations. You run a highly professional establishment."

She shifted, avoiding his stare to hide her discomfiture. He'd been referring to the restaurant and not her when he'd said *nice*.

She ushered him to a table by the mullioned window where he stood while she hunted for the catering menus. Not only was she not exuding professionalism, she hadn't had time to prepare properly for their meeting.

Thrilled to find the menus on a vacant chair, she displayed them. "You've never dined here before?"

"The opportunity never came up, although a number of my friends eat here often and sing your praises. Your website is excellent too, and extremely user friendly. I thoroughly checked every detail." It was on the tip of her tongue to ask him why he hadn't used her website to book his reservation, but then he grinned and continued, "You're much prettier in person than the picture of you on your website."

This time his flattery was specifically meant for her. She took a moment to digest his compliment and decided the best response was a simple "Thank you."

In any case, her photo on The Pasta Junction's website was a few years old. Lorenzo might be admiring her, but in truth he was probably disillusioned upon seeing her in person.

She was ten years younger in the photo which had been taken when she'd first purchased the restaurant. She'd worn a form-fitting white dress, her makeup professionally done to emphasize her blue eyes, her face powdered to a porcelain finish. Her trademark fedora hat was slanted to one side.

"Blond hair, expressive eyes …" Lorenzo was saying. "And your old-school Hollywood style is lovely. You exude under-stated elegance."

Hold on. Had he said lovely? Understated elegance?

Yes, both. He'd said both. *The charisma of an Italian man.*

She considered setting him in his place once and for all. Compliments were appreciated, but he was married. Hastily, she reminded herself that this was a business meeting, and he was a customer.

Keep the conversation efficient and quick.

"My restaurant has been open for ten years," she replied. "That's an old photo of me on the website."

"You haven't changed."

Her cheeks were most likely flaming scarlet by now, shining through the translucent powder. She smoothed her shirt, adjusted the collar. "Hardly."

"And I can't believe I've never dined here," he said.

She offered a polite smile. He reciprocated the smile, then shifted to stare out the window at passing traffic. Across the street, a sparkly gold Christmas angel hanging on a lamppost whipped in a gust of wind.

The restaurant was located in a revitalized area of Bloomingfield that featured, among other attractions, a café, bookstore and antique shop. All the buildings were brick, and a steepled white church and covered bridge in the distance completed the idyllic small-town atmosphere.

"Is that yours?" She gestured to a sporty SUV parked in front of her restaurant.

"Yes."

The SUV looked brand new. Evidently, he was generously paid at the television station.

He seemed to notice her appraisal of him, of the car, and pounced on an explanation. "Any degree of success in the broadcasting arena comes with a tall ladder to climb."

She nodded. They both stared outdoors again.

The weather was a typical morning in winter—chilly, windy and rainy. Julie didn't mind. She liked the rain, the scent of wet leaves and grass, the coolness of a clean breeze. Besides, in California the sunshine was likely to stream through the clouds before the day was over.

While Lorenzo stood quiet, she studied his profile—his straight nose and well-carved features. He could have stepped out of a Tuscany painting, and she visualized him laboring in a vineyard, his face streaked with dirt. Beneath his polished television exterior and three-piece suits, there was definitely a ruggedness that went beyond his solid masculinity.

She gave herself a firm mental scolding. What was she doing, fantasizing about a married man?

She yanked her thoughts back to the present and to business.

An eye-catching weatherman who fluttered hearts every night on television might attract other women, but this man was entirely off limits.

"I forgot my manners." His gaze shifted from the window to her and he extended his hand. "I appreciate you taking an hour out of your hectic schedule."

She wiped her hands on her slacks, hoping the garlic odor had been washed away, and accepted his handshake. His fingers were warm and strong and strangely callused for a man who worked indoors and studied weather charts.

"I'm delighted to help you plan your special event," she said with a smile.

Something glimmered in his gaze, and he held her hand for a second longer than she expected. "A successful woman like yourself must be extremely busy this time of year."

Wow, he was an enchanter.

"I am, and I'm grateful for the busyness." The feel of his hand stirred a tingling sensation, and she yanked it away. She kept her smile, but refined it to a cool and distant one. "Will you take coffee, Lorenzo? Or cappuccino?"

He shrugged off his jacket and draped it over a chair. "Is your coffee served with a traditional flaky pastry like they serve in Italy?"

"I didn't know flaky pastries were customary there." His question sidetracked her. "Have you ever visited?"

"Often. I inherited an ancient ancestral home in Calitri. My parents moved to America when I was quite young. They are Italian immigrants."

"Your home must be beautiful."

"A century ago, it probably was. Now, the stone is decaying, and it's no longer livable, so I purchased a modest apartment in the center of town." He gazed at her. "Have you ever visited Italy?" he asked again.

"No. Hopefully, someday."

"Someday." He smiled. "Someday, we all hope to accomplish a great many things."

What, exactly, did that mean? Did he have dreams he hadn't yet fulfilled, or was he referring to people in general? Or her?

No, definitely not her. He hardly knew her.

"Well, do you?" he was asking.

"Do I what?"

"Have any flaky pastries on hand?"

Not until she hired the new pastry chef, she almost told him. Instead, she answered, "Today I'm serving biscotti with your coffee." Fortunately, the restaurant had a score of the crunchy almond cookies packed airtight in the kitchen.

His thoughtful gaze continued to study her, and she self-consciously twirled a pin curl.

He grinned. "I'll stick with coffee Americano, though I expect your biscotti is delicious."

Yes, definitely a charmer.

An awkward beat passed. "Sugar and cream?" she asked.

"Black."

"Me too." She set down the menus. In the kitchen, she poured two cups of coffee and brought them to the table.

"Are you interested in seeing the separate room we use for parties?" She nodded toward the cocktail lounge. "It's decorated the same as the main dining room."

"Nope. I'm sure it's ideal." He was standing precisely where she'd left him. His jeans looked faded and the gray T-shirt, emblazoned with the words Trust Me, I Know Everything About the Weather, enhanced his muscled, tanned physique.

"I love the smell of coffee," he said softly.

She swallowed and offered a brief affirmation. His manner was unassuming, his compelling blue eyes bringing to mind an impossibly blue sky. And interest. Unmistakable interest.

Why? Wasn't this a celebratory dinner for his wife?

The knowledge gave Julie pause, and she stepped back. Charmer or not, this type of man wasn't at all to her liking.

She placed the coffees on the table and slid onto a wooden chair.

He grabbed a seat across from her and sipped his coffee. "Excellent. You can always determine the quality of a restaurant by the coffee."

"Among other things," she murmured.

"Needless to say, the meal is important too."

"And the atmosphere."

"Right."

"And the freshness of the food."

"Point taken." He held up his hands. "I summarized the entire restaurant business to a cup of coffee, when there's plenty more to consider." He leaned forward. "Care to enlighten me on the successful approach to running a restaurant? From personal knowledge, it's an expensive venture."

"You owned a restaurant?" she asked.

Feigning interest in the crystal salt and pepper shakers in the middle of the table, he replied, "Nothing hands-on."

Was he making small talk? How much should she elaborate, because she could converse for hours about her restaurant.

"I'm interested in creating fine cuisine." She steepled her fingers. "I leave the actual operation to my accounting manager. He specializes in the food industry, and before I employed him my invoices were a muddled mess. Attention to detail isn't my forte."

"I'm all about detail, which is why I'm here."

"I understand." She slid the menus across the table. "Please take a look. We offer numerous selections to accommodate the most discerning diner, at a cost suitable for every budget."

"You sound like a commercial."

"I'm a businesswoman."

He took a swallow of coffee, and so did she. His gaze skimmed the menus before he set them aside. "Why don't you choose?"

"Me?" She eyed him over the rim of her cup. "I don't presume to know your tastes."

"Probably not in food," he replied. "But you can make an educated guess about my other tastes."

Surely he wasn't coming on to her again.

Ignoring his remark, she pointedly stacked the menus from appetizer to entrees and pushed them back toward him. "I suggest trays of meatballs, baked chicken, and pasta for your main dishes."

"Whatever you think best."

"Or you might prefer a plated sit-down, which is more expensive. However, then each guest can choose whichever entrée they wish."

He shook his head. "Let's avoid the whole perusal of the menu thing."

Perusal of the menu thing? Wasn't he planning this dinner?

Julie kept her chin high. "May I ask why?"

"All that negotiating—who's ordering which entrée and side dishes—takes time."

"Perhaps consider a limited menu with fewer selections?"

Another head shake. "Too distracting."

"Part of the fun of going out to eat is the cuisine choices."

"For me, the importance of a meal is family and friends sharing the experience together." His sincere smile revealed the dimple on his chin, and her heart did a turn. She almost excused herself to scurry into the kitchen so that she could draw a deep breath and collect herself.

Whenever she'd watched his weather reports, she assumed the camera, lighting, and makeup enhanced his good looks. He couldn't be *that* attractive in person.

But he was.

His thick black hair was shiny, with glints of golden brown at the temples. The warmth in his tone as he talked about friends and family prompted her to nod her head in agreement. Time spent with the people you loved was what mattered most.

His reply was a lazy smile.

Her cheeks burned, and she tamped down the hazardous leap in her pulse. She was staring at him with an expression befitting a sixteen-year-old.

She sat straighter and focused on the stack of menus. *All right, Mr. handsome Two-Timing Meteorologist. Back to business.*

"How about a buffet?" she suggested. "We can serve the typical Italian fare of meatballs in a marinara sauce, a tray of my signature fettuccini, sausage and peppers, baked chicken, and garlic bread." She numbered the selections with her fingers. "That way, no one needs to spend a second on any food decisions. We'll set up the buffet on a side table and guests can help themselves."

His gaze flicked over the menus. "Sounds good." For a guy so focused on details, her list of options didn't seem to hold his attention for long. "Don't forget Grandma Gloria's cassata for dessert."

"Did you bring the recipe?"

"Indeed." He reached into his jacket pocket and handed

her a folded sheet of paper. "I'd never forget such an important feature of the party."

Along with his stunning wife, Julie thought. She darted a glance at his left hand. He wasn't wearing a wedding band, but many men didn't, and he'd mentioned he was reporting to the television studio afterwards. Perhaps he had a rule of not wearing jewelry on the air.

Or perhaps he was a double-crossing cad who flirted with women regardless of his marital status.

She unfolded the yellowed paper and perused the directions. Nothing too difficult. In fact, the recipe called for a basic cake mix found in any supermarket. Nonetheless, everything was handwritten, and the ingredients were listed in vague amounts. Her kind of recipe, without numerous restrictions.

"Offhand, do you know how many people the recipe serves?" she asked.

"You're the cook."

"Haven't you eaten this dessert before?"

He sighed and rubbed a hand on his heart. "When I was young, I remember my grandmother preparing the cheesecake for special family occasions."

He didn't answer her question, but Julie let it pass.

His cell phone buzzed, and he pulled it out of his pocket and looked at the caller ID. With an apology to Julie for the interruption, he answered the call.

"Hey, yes, Regina, I'm meeting with the owner right now." Lorenzo laughed. "I don't have a crystal ball, only Doppler radar, so I can't answer your weather question. I'll text you later. *Ciao*." He disconnected, tucked the phone into his pocket and gave a rueful shrug. "That was my sister joking about my storm prediction last month."

"You mean the storm that never materialized?"

He glanced out the window, then back at her. "Aren't you glad I was wrong?"

"Absolutely, but ...your warning flashed across my phone screen and unnerved me. I debated whether to close my restaurant or remain open."

"I take it you didn't close?"

She bit back a smirk. "No, but I did close early."

"Wait." He grinned. "You subscribe to my weather app?"

"Doesn't everyone in town? Your presence is well known."

A flicker of annoyance, or something she couldn't determine, caused him to look away. "I've asked the television station to ease up on advertising, but the studio managers are obsessed with high ratings. I can't argue. They're right about social media."

"I focus my advertising on the newspaper and my website," Julie said.

"You're missing limitless opportunities. Technology is the key to a successful operation, including a restaurant."

"You seem to know a lot about the restaurant business."

"Some." His tone became subdued. "Regarding technology and my forecasting, I heed the advice of my station managers. They're the experts."

She propped her chin on her hands. "You're admitting that your breathless melodramas during storm coverages are over hyped?"

"Whoa, you get right to the point."

"Twice, I almost closed because of your severe storm watch. You made it sound as if disaster was imminent, and I should rush to the grocery store and purchase all the bottled water on the shelves." She kept her posture rigid. "The first time, I actually did. This time, I thought better."

"So you disregarded my forecast." His voice deepened. "Why would you put your patrons in danger?"

"A watch means a storm *may* occur."

"Very good. And a warning means conditions are imminent. So again, why not heed a meteorologist's advice?"

"Because you tend to be wrong more than you're right." She twisted a button on her sleeve. "I'm sorry, I didn't mean to sound negative. We joke about your forecasts ... sometimes."

"You joke ..." Through narrowed eyes, he studied her. "Who are *we*?"

"Employees, friends, family—"

"On a seven-day forecast, I'm right 80 percent of the time."

"How about a five-day forecast?"

He took a gulp of coffee. "Ninety percent."

"Ten-day?"

"Now you're pushing it." He leaned back and folded his arms. "I'm right half the time on a ten-day. Long-range forecasts are challenging because there are numerous variables." He peered at his watch. "At any rate, I'm not here to discuss the weather."

"And your forecast for today is ...?"

He grinned and gestured outside, where raindrops bucketed down. "Rainy."

She shared his grin and then, reminding herself there was business to be discussed, asked if the people coming to the dinner were local.

"My sister Regina lives here in Bloomingfield. Be prepared, though." He grimaced. "Her twin girls, Ella and Emma, are adorable but mischievous."

"I can handle mischievous."

"How about energetic?"

"That too. How old are the girls?"

"Seven." He rolled his eyes. "Their favorite activities are jumping off things and chasing each other."

Julie laughed. "Typical child behavior. So how many

people in your party, total?"

"There's Regina, my brother-in-law, and their twin daughters, and my brother John in Wyoming. He's not married. Altogether," Lorenzo finished, "we're eight people. That includes my mother and her husband, of course."

"Of course." Julie skimmed the recipe again. "The cassata recipe is manageable, plus it gives me leeway."

"Leeway to do what?"

"Leeway to experiment." Noting his frown, she continued, "I'll double the recipe to ensure there'll be enough for everyone, and extra to take home."

"I'd like a replica."

"Yes, so you've said. I'll do my best," Julie replied. "Just as there are variables in predicting the weather, the same holds true for baked goods. Cassata consists of ricotta cheese and chocolate and cherries, and these ingredients react differently to oven temperatures. In fact, sometimes it all boils down to what factory the boxed cake mix came from."

"If you measure every ingredient exactly, it should taste the same as my grandmother's."

She pointed to the scribbles on the recipe. "A pinch of this and a little of that isn't exact. Besides, each person's taste isn't the same. Baking is subjective."

"Baking is all about measuring the ingredients correctly and accurately," he said. "Unfortunately, my mother wasn't much of a baker and always failed to recreate her mother's prized dessert. Fortunately, you are an excellent cook."

He didn't know that for certain. He hadn't even eaten at her restaurant. He just assumed she was a good cook because her restaurant was successful.

She shifted. "Is your grandmother still alive?"

"Sadly, no. She passed many years ago. She never spoke a word of English and insisted I only speak Italian when I was with her." He offered a stoic shrug. "When you lose someone special in your life, you come to realize you miss them more with each passing day."

"A dear cousin of mine moved away," Julie responded. "We used to go to the cinema together on Monday afternoon."

"What did you see?" he asked.

"See where?"

"At the cinema. What were your favorite movies?"

"You probably never heard of them."

"Try me."

"Just black and white films. Filled with flashbacks and stark lighting."

Slowly, he nodded. "Film noir."

"You recognize the term?"

"Certainly. I like it too. The run-down Grover Theater features those old movies."

"I haven't been there since my cousin moved away."

He caught her gaze and held it. "Sometimes film noir movies are pessimistic."

"Sometimes not." She savored her coffee. Even cold, it was good. "Usually, the heroes are cynical."

"Do you like cynical heroes?"

"I prefer guys who are genuinely good, honest, and sincere." Although she hadn't met a man with those qualities and oftentimes wondered if such a man truly existed.

She flashed a glimpse at Lorenzo, who was considering her intently. Another reason why she had pledged not to date again. Because of two-timing cads like him.

And yet, her endless hours devoted to her restaurant had led to worried discussions with her brother, Ben, and her sisters, Sally and Katie, who had all told Julie her apartment was too lonely. She'd placated their concerns by promising to get a dog, although when a dog might happen was beyond her.

Maybe when the new year started ...

"All the actors in film noir movies are smokers," Lorenzo wrapped his hands around his coffee cup. Sturdy and firm hands, she noticed. "Do you?"

"Do I smoke? I own a cigarette holder. Does that count?"

He laughed. "Nope."

"Then no." She shook her head. "You?"

"Not me, although my grandmother did. I remember spending rainy afternoons baking with her. She'd take a cigarette break every so often, and she always smoked outdoors no matter the weather. The aromas of chocolate and cherries coming from her kitchen when her cassata was in the oven are some of my best memories."

"Along with cigarette smoke?' Julie teased.

"Chesterfield."

"I had an aunt who smoked Chesterfield cigarettes too."

She paused, considering the pensive look on his face before he regarded the yellowed recipe. It seemed as if he sought to replicate the joyful times he'd spent with his grandmother, the satisfying aromas and pleasant feelings, and not the actual cheesecake.

Julie kept the thought to herself, although it was becoming clear that the recipe's relevance to this anniversary was no coincidence.

"This cassata is important to me," he said, "because it's important to my mother. I want it to be perfect for her. She went through a lot when my father died, and she's finally found happiness."

"I'm glad for her," Julie said, puzzled.

"Me too." Again, he smiled. Again, his blue eyes glinted with undisguised attraction.

And again, she stiffened. The eyes, the flirty smile. Where was he going with this?

Good-natured laughter sounded from the kitchen, meaning the waitstaff was arriving.

She tapped her heels, then pushed back her chair and stood.

Lorenzo came instantly to his feet. "I want to taste the cassata you bake before the actual event."

"I assumed so. However, my waking hours between now and the beginning of January are jam-packed."

Briefly, he touched her arm. Again, the tingle. Again, she pulled back.

"I'll pay you for your efforts," he said. "I don't expect you to work for free."

She picked up the menus. "It's not so much the money, it's the time."

"I'm hoping you can squeeze me into your schedule."

Right.

His statement began with a hope, but sounded suspiciously like a demand.

With a sigh, she mulled over their mutual interest in film noir, black coffee, their shared fondness of fine food. And sure, the Chesterfield cigarettes.

"Less than two weeks before New Year's ..." she muttered, half to herself.

"I'm visiting my mother and stepfather in Wyoming for Christmas. They live near my brother and the big excitement of the trip is the holiday concert with the Wyoming Symphony Orchestra. We're all big symphony lovers."

"I love full orchestras. Over a decade ago, I played the violin." Now why was she telling him more personal information about herself? If she spent another minute with this man, she'd be pouring out her life story.

"I was first chair trumpet in the high school band," he said.

"Are you bragging?"

He laughed. "No. Well, yes, maybe I was, but by my senior year I became more fascinated by the weather than the band.

So I quit, much to my music teacher's dismay." He kept her gaze. "You?"

"Much the same, although my teacher was probably thrilled because I hardly ever practiced. By then, my attention shifted to fine cuisine and experimenting with recipes."

"It seems we share a number of commonalities."

She forced herself to keep her attention on the menus clutched in her hand.

"At any rate," he went on, "I'll be back in Bloomingfield the day after Christmas. May I contact you then?"

"Phone the restaurant to schedule a taste test, but allow me a few hours' lead time."

If he caught on that her reply was evasive he made no mention, nor did he press for her personal cellphone number.

"I'll look forward to our first cassata sampling together," he said.

"First?"

"Unless you get it right."

"I will."

He smiled. "We'll see."

She walked him to the front door, and he gestured to her fedora, still drying on the coat rack. "Fine hat."

"Thanks."

"Well, Merry Christmas, Julie." With a nod, he departed.

"Merry Christmas, Lorenzo," she said as the door swung closed behind him.

She'd spend another lonely Christmas working. He'd settle in at the symphony, listening to classical music and relaxing with his family and wife.

CHAPTER THREE

The perfect dessert.

Julie grabbed an oven mitt and removed an exquisitely baked cassata from the oven. Pleased with herself, she eyed the smooth, even texture as she set it on the stainless-steel cooktop in her restaurant's kitchen.

It was the Monday after Christmas, the only day The Pasta Junction was closed. Although weary from the flow of never-ending diners on Christmas Eve and Christmas Day, she was satisfied. Profits were excellent, and her employees had been pleased with big-hearted tips from customers and the year-end bonus Julie annually presented. She and her staff were a team, and the addition of several new waiters had lessened the job strain.

However, the search for a proficient pastry chef had yielded no results, and she continued to outsource her desserts to a local bakery.

To be sure, Lorenzo would have none of it.

With a quiet groan, she reflected on their last phone conversation. He'd rung the restaurant on Christmas Eve, apparently timing his call for when she closed at ten o'clock.

"I wanted to wish you a Merry Christmas, Julie," he said. "Will you be able to spend any time with your family?"

"My brother, Ben, and Maise stopped in for a late dinner tonight. She's a new food editor in town, and Ben co-owns Bloomingfield Candy Shop, along with my sister Sally. Their shop won first place in a chocolate contest."

"Yes, I remember reading the article in the newspaper."

"If you're ever in the market for the finest chocolate in Bloomingfield, be sure to visit."

"Chocolate is a weakness of mine, and so is ..." She waited, half-expecting him to rattle off his favorite fudge flavor, but silence sat in the open and he didn't elaborate.

Naturally, they chatted about the weather and then the holiday, before the subject veered to Lorenzo's upcoming party.

"I'll arrive in Bloomingfield the day after Christmas," he said. "Can we arrange a time to meet?"

"To taste test the cassata, you mean."

"Right."

"It might be better to assign the cassata to a true baker," she said. "I'm in the process of looking for a pastry chef. In the meantime, the bakery my restaurant outsources to is excellent, and your recipe is easy."

"I want only the best restauranteur in Bloomingfield to prepare it." His response was swift and firm. "And please wish your brother and sisters a Merry Christmas from me and my family."

Apparently that was the conclusion of their discussion.

They set a day and time, agreed to meet at her restaurant, exchanged Merry Christmases, and clicked off.

. . .

nd that day and time had arrived on a rainy Monday morning.

Julie cast a critical appraisal of herself in her restaurant's full-length mirror. A couple days had passed since she'd spoken with Lorenzo, and she couldn't control her thoughts about him—his friendly smiles, the deep timbre of his voice.

She'd run late, as usual, and opted for casual clothes—dark skinny jeans and a vintage T-shirt—her makeup a raisin-colored lipstick and porcelain finishing powder. She'd brushed her hair into soft waves, rolling it to the side in a bun and pinning it in place.

She perched on a stool in the restaurant kitchen, massaging her temples and rereading the recipe. The directions and ingredients were unclear, so she'd taken some liberties. Being a chocoholic, she preferred a larger quantity of chocolate and a smaller amount of maraschino cherries.

A soft knock on the front door had her hurrying to the entrance.

Lorenzo stood in the doorway, tall and handsome, his captivating blue eyes holding her gaze. His broad shoulders filled out his gray trench coat to perfection. The other day, he looked as if he could have been toiling in an olive field. Today, he resembled a man who had just stepped off the set of film noir. All he lacked was a dimly lit bar, and a foggy evening.

Her heart skipped a beat which seemed to be the recent norm when it came to Lorenzo Rossi.

"Hi, Julie." He grinned and brandished an oversized tube in the air. "I bought you something."

She ushered him inside. "Why?"

"Because it's Christmas."

"Lorenzo, thank you. I didn't buy you anything."

"You're the key to my successful party, which is a magnificent gift in itself." He regarded her with frank admiration. "And you look beautiful on this lovely California day."

"It's another rainy day." She gazed outside, listening to the gentle tapping of raindrops on the sidewalk.

"I like the rain and take comfort in it," he said. "For me, it's relaxing. And you are beautiful."

Self-conscious because he'd repeated his compliment, Julie adjusted her white apron and murmured a thank you.

Beautiful was a term no one used to describe her. Attractive, cute and pretty, but never beautiful, though she had been blessed with her mother's high cheekbones and plump lips. Nonetheless, when Julie peered at herself in the mirror, the woman who stared back at her looked stressed, in a never-ending cycle of work that defined her life.

"I discovered a quaint boutique in Wyoming, and thought of you," Lorenzo said. He pulled off his coat and slung it over his shoulder. Again, he wore a T-shirt and jeans that looked comfortable and lived-in, yet emphasized his strong physique.

"You shouldn't have bought me anything. We hardly know each other."

"But I did, because I hope to get to know you better." He handed her the tube and stepped to an empty table. "I'm hoping you'll hang my gift in your kitchen."

Should she? She wondered, viewing the oversized tube with uncertainty.

Why not? she argued with herself and then backtracked.

Understandably, it depended on the poster. If it was suitable for her restaurant, perhaps an inspiring photo depicting Italian pastries, then the gift wasn't personal.

"Go on," Lorenzo prodded, gesturing her to stand next to him. "I want to see you smile when you open it."

Her curiosity piqued, she arranged the poster on the table and unrolled it.

And then she smiled. And so did he.

The black and white poster portrayed a woman wearing a black dress, fedora, and shiny lipstick.

But it was the words on the poster that prompted Julie to step back.

A beautiful woman has strolled into my peaceful life.

"Do you like it?" he asked.

"Are you joking?" Her smile died. "Lorenzo, I can't possibly accept this."

"Why not?"

"The words are too ... too personal."

"And that's because ...?"

She folded her hands together and frowned. "To begin with, what about your wife?" It hurt to even say the words aloud, because Julie's pulse kicked up a notch every minute she looked at him. But she'd heard the old adage and agreed with it: *The truth hurts, but it's better than an untruth*.

Eyes wide with astonishment, he stared at her. "What wife?"

"The woman you wed a year ago?" Julie's lips pursed. "Mrs. Rossi? The reason you're planning this fabulous party?"

He chuckled. Chuckled of all things. "You're right. There was a Mrs. Rossi."

"So consequently—"

"Consequently ..." His blue eyes gleamed with mirth. "Consequently there was a Mrs. Rossi before my mother remarried, but now her name is Mrs. Talley."

"I'm not referring to your mother." Julie's tone sharpened. "I'm referring to your wife."

Her statement seemed to amuse him all the more. "Whatever gave you that idea? I'm not married."

"You're not ..." For the first time since he'd spoken, his response finally penetrated her brain. "Then who is this party for?"

"My mother and her husband, my stepfather, Joe Talley. I

spent the holiday with them and managed to keep their surprise a secret, which was difficult because I'm terrible at keeping secrets. My sister invited them to Bloomingfield for New Year's Day to celebrate their first anniversary, which is how this party all came together." He paused. "Did you think I was flirting with you even though I was married?" He shook his head and scowled. "I see from your expression that's exactly what you thought."

A slice of guilt pierced her. She'd fixed him on an imaginary jury stand and judged him guilty without the facts. No wonder he was scowling.

"The thought crossed my mind," she said quietly. "I apologize."

"Apology accepted on one condition." His tone was so reasonable, she nearly consented without hearing what the condition was.

Nearly consented.

"Which is?" she asked.

"You'll smile and accept my gift."

"I already smiled."

"I'll wait for your smile again when you hang the poster in your kitchen."

"My entire staff will click their tongues for a year if I hang this poster in there." She gestured toward the kitchen.

"I wasn't referring to your restaurant kitchen. I was hoping you'd bring the poster home."

With him? Was that what he was implying?

"I'll think about it," she hedged. "But what are you trying to say? These words are ..."

His gaze slid tellingly from the poster to her face. "You know exactly what I'm saying, although the poster states the fact better than I do."

She felt a rosy blush tinting her cheeks and tried to make light of his comment with a nod. "Thank you," she whispered, pondering the madness that seemed to overtake her whenever Lorenzo was near.

"You're forgetting to smile," he reminded.

She managed a grin, and his gaze softened.

"From the delicious aroma I smelled as soon as I walked in, I presume you've been baking." He extended his hand. "Shall we begin our first taste test?"

She accepted and led the way to the kitchen. "The cheesecake isn't cool enough to cut yet," she warned.

"How long?"

She couldn't resist teasing him. "Oh, we'll probably have to wait three or four hours."

He tilted his head. "I'll phone the station to tell them I'll be late. I'm not on television until the six o'clock news."

Would he really stay for cheesecake? Or was it more ... perhaps to spend more time with her?

"Lorenzo, I'm joking." They were still holding hands. Quickly, she let go.

He set his coat on a stool, then removed his cell phone from his jeans pocket. "How long, then?"

"Probably an hour, although the cheesecake is heavy and thick, so possibly longer."

He quirked a dark eyebrow and grinned. "I have time if you do."

There were a million matters calling for her attention, but spending an extra hour with this captivating man was suddenly more important.

He pulled out a stool by the counter for her. "I planned to work in my office, but my job can wait," he said.

"My job never can." She glanced at the coffee maker. She must order a new grinder soon. And she still lacked a pastry chef.

She eyed leftover dough sitting on a tray near a workstation. Perhaps she'd spin it into pizza. If so, she was forced to use her conventional oven, though she'd recently considered purchasing a brick pizza oven.

She shifted to Lorenzo. "Maise, the new food critic, reviewed my restaurant in the newspaper."

"Yes, I read the article."

Julie nodded. At first, Maise's article had upset Julie, but then she'd pondered Maise's suggestion and was seriously considering it.

"Maise was surprised The Pasta Junction didn't serve pizza," she said.

"I thought the same. Because this is an Italian restaurant. I assumed pizza was on your menu."

"The Pasta Junction is high-end, not a corner pizzeria. They have an entirely different clientele."

"Do they?" he asked. "Everyone likes pizza, even the fancy clientele."

"Like you?"

"I may come across as posh on television because I wear a three-piece suit. But believe me, I'm a regular, stay-at-home kind of guy."

Julie tapped her fingers and pushed out a breath. He and Maise were probably correct about serving pizza, and no doubt a variety of pizzas with different toppings—pepperoni, assorted vegetables, grilled chicken—would quickly become restaurant favorites.

She grabbed her laptop computer from its shelf and flipped it open. "A pizza oven is the first step." Intent on her task, she surfed the internet before pointing to the screen. "This oven is top notch, but it costs ten thousand dollars."

"Wow. You'll need to sell a lot of pizzas to make a profit." Lorenzo reached for his glasses in his pocket and put them on. "Did you calculate the cost of labor and ingredients?"

"Several times, and the price comes out to approximately six dollars per pizza."

"Can't you outsource pizzas like you outsource desserts?"

"Outsourcing desserts is temporary," she reminded as she viewed the computer screen. The oven price was prohibitive. However, she could charge by the slice. Two dollars per slice and eight servings in one pizza equaled ...

She fiddled with a pin that came loose from her bun. Somewhere in the back of her head, a headache began to erupt. Stress seemed to produce that more and more lately, along with a constant money worry.

"Are you a workaholic?" Lorenzo asked, interrupting her reflections. His gaze was probing yet caring, and some of her frustration evaporated.

"My siblings, Ben and Sally and Katie, certainly think I am. Still, Sally is as driven as I am. She throws every bit of effort into her chocolate shop."

"Perhaps you might consider less time on the job or more people to share your workload? Did any of your siblings offer a solution?"

"Yes, and they also suggested I get a dog."

His lips rounded into a smile. "A dog offers unconditional love. What type are you considering?"

"*I'm* not considering a dog. *They* are. For me."

"Big or little? If you have allergies—"

"I told you, no dog. I can't devote the care he might need."

"He?"

"*If* I ever get a dog, which I'm not, I've considered naming him Buddy."

"I'm partial to beagles. I'm available any time if you want to stop by the local animal shelter." He acted as if he hadn't heard her. "There are countless animals begging to be adopted."

Her legs were tired from standing, and Lorenzo's unswerving gaze flustered her. He was looking for an assurance that she would visit the animal shelter with him, and she couldn't guarantee it. Besides, she didn't want to leave a dog alone for extended periods while she worked.

For lack of anything else to say, she asked Lorenzo if he would like a cup of coffee.

He leaned against the counter. "Will the coffee be as good as the other day?"

"Absolutely not." She cut her gaze to the overworked coffee machine. "This coffee has sat out for a couple hours. It might taste stale, but I can brew a fresh pot."

"I'm easy. Old coffee works for me."

Easy about coffee maybe, but certainly not about his grandmother's recipe.

She went to the coffeemaker and poured him a cup, then lifted the lid of a glass bin overflowing with biscotti. "The cookies are hard, but excellent for dunking in a hot drink."

"Or breaking a tooth." He sipped the coffee she set beside him and slightly grimaced. "Considering the coffee is lukewarm, I better not take my chances."

She grinned. "You might look odd on television with a missing front tooth."

"It wouldn't be the first time."

She blinked. Her lips parted. "You're kidding, right?"

"Nope." He pulled in a breath. "Before I worked in Bloomingfield, I was a weatherman at a prestigious Atlanta television station. In college, I'd decided on a dual degree in meteorology and journalism, and began my career in smaller markets. After several years, I was hired as the anchor weatherman on the evening news. Finally, I thought, I'm in a big city and snagged my dream job. Everything was ideal. At least, so I assumed."

"And?"

"I'd worked at the station three years. One afternoon, I

had a run-in with a guy who had been my best friend at college."

"Your friend came into the television station to speak with you?"

"Yes, on a business matter that ended up being personal. He'd needed help, and I'd given it." Lorenzo pressed his lips together. "Our conversation escalated to a disagreement, and he punched me in the jaw."

"Why? What was the business matter?"

"I'd lent him some money, which apparently wasn't enough, because he wanted more. I refused, and he wasn't happy."

"The personal matter?"

"My supposed girlfriend who was actually dating both of us." He refused to meet her stare. "During our heated disagreement, I lost a tooth. After my TV segment was over, I was served my walking papers. It was wrong of me to argue publicly with him, especially at my job."

"Who threw the first punch?"

"He did. I threw the second. There were only two."

She bit her lip. "Who broke up the fight?"

"The station manager." Lorenzo shook his head. "Honestly, none of this matters. The primary requirement in media is to present an accomplished image, and I failed."

"You were trying to protect yourself."

"I've never struck anyone in my life, either before or after that incident. It was instinctive, but it was wrong."

A silence filled the air. Lorenzo had owned up to his mistake. In summary, he'd been stripped of his job and title because of it. Still, admitting wrongness took courage and conviction.

Julie waited a beat until his gaze rested on her. He gave a heavy sigh.

"What happened doesn't seem fair." Her tone softened.

"Your supposed friend was clearly looking for a fight. Losing your dream job must have been devastating."

Lorenzo took off his eyeglasses and rubbed his eyes. "In the end, it was for the best. I found a job I love here in Bloomingfield, and because the town is small, the hours aren't as demanding. The managers matched my Atlanta salary, so I'm not complaining. Thus, I can pursue other interests, like baking." He chucked her under the chin.

"Uh-huh." She smiled. "As if you like to bake."

"I'm starting to enjoy baking a great deal." He leaned over and pressed a light kiss on her mouth. His lips were warm, the flavor of dark coffee.

She should have pulled away. Instead, her heart did a little flip in her chest.

"Truthfully," he whispered, "I'm growing fonder and fonder of ..."

"Baking?"

"Spending time with you."

"Lorenzo," she murmured, "I'm not interested in dating."

"Surely a woman—"

"A *businesswoman*. The restaurant is always on my mind, and I don't have room in my life for anyone or anything else." She drew away and didn't meet his gaze.

Such a feathery, brief kiss, but it had been perilously comfortable, as if they had kissed before and would again.

No, no. This entire cassata taste testing was a bad idea. She couldn't get entangled in a relationship. *Wouldn't* get entangled in a relationship. Determinedly, she erected the safe barricade around her heart and reverted to her practical self.

"I have no flaky pastry to offer you today, either. Sorry."

"How about a bottle of water?" he asked.

"Certainly." A quick reach in the cooler, and she placed the water beside him.

"Thanks." He downed the water. "Someday, I'd like you to come to Italy with me to savor the finest pastry in the world."

She hesitated. He was full of surprises.

He observed her closely, as if interested in her response.

"Are you offering an invitation?" she asked.

He grinned. "Of the most blatant kind."

"I've never flown." Her explanation came out more like an embarrassed confession than an excuse.

"Are you afraid?"

"The opportunity never presented itself. When I was young, my parents hardly traveled. And the past few years I've been trying to succeed in this challenging restaurant business."

"Are you … succeeding?"

"Sometimes yes." She sagged onto the stool, a kaleido-scope of stressful nights filing through her mind. "Sometimes no. The workload is tremendous."

He sat beside her. "Are you enjoying your life?"

"I can't get philosophical in the daytime."

"Good excuse, and even more of a reason that you deserve a break." He reached out to take her hands, his grip firm and reassuring. "If it's your first experience, you might as well fly with someone you trust."

"I never consented to go with you. Furthermore, I'm supposed to trust you? These are early days in our friendship."

"Yes, we're definitely friends, Julie, and I'm hoping we'll become more than friends. I find you truly amazing."

She was in new territory, too fresh and unfamiliar, and she didn't know whether to respond with a smile or a scoff.

"I've always dreamed of seeing Italy," she murmured. "It's just not possible between my restaurant and financial demands."

"Since you own an Italian restaurant, you can draw upon

old-country techniques and innovative recipes, so it's a business trip. I visit my relatives there often."

"Is that why you're inviting me? To help me improve my business?"

"Yes, and because, as you stated, we are friends."

Just two friends traveling to Italy together.

She envisioned the scenario. Warm Mediterranean sunshine, scents of olives and garlic, appreciating the gorgeous architecture, dining on local cuisine every day.

She swallowed the knot in her throat, conscious of her tight schedule and realizing she'd never be able to visit. Going forward, she would be wise to keep that cold realization in her mind when dealing with Lorenzo. They were two experts in their fields, and this was a business relationship.

"But in the meantime, my *friend,* while we're here in California?" She tugged her hands from his, rolled to her feet and motioned toward the tin. "Would you like a biscotti?"

"I'm set. Thanks." He glanced at the stovetop. "I'm a patient man."

"I was late getting the cassata in the oven, and when I inserted a knife to check if it came out clean, it didn't. So I left the cheesecake in for another ten minutes."

"Is that good or bad?"

"We'll see." She refilled his coffee cup and perched on the stool. "So, what should we chat about while we wait for the cassata to cool?"

He had stood when she did. Now he propped on his stool once more, his feet resting on the bottom rung. "The weather?"

She laughed. "No sensationalism for New Year's Eve, I hope?"

"I returned to Bloomingfield a short time ago. Tune in to my segment tonight to hear the complete forecast."

"Because I'm a busy restaurant owner, I might not have time." She flashed him a smile. "Although I'll try."

Oh, she'd do more than try. Lorenzo's funny, endearing style captivated her. He made the weather forecast humorous, almost as if he told a story each night. She said as much and received a satisfied grin in reply. "Thank you, Julie. Your kind words mean a lot to me."

CHAPTER FOUR

*L*orenzo drank more of his water, forcing himself not to stare at the striking woman sitting next to him. Her sparkling gaze and sweet smile made his pulse race.

He slanted her a glance, unsurprised that she had switched into businesslike mode again. Already, he was beginning to know her.

They sat so near their knees touched, and his heartbeat accelerated. Julie's face was as close to perfection as any woman he'd ever seen, especially when she smiled.

He'd examined several restaurants' websites when he was first organizing this anniversary party. It was his way of showing his mother he approved of her new relationship, and that by marrying Joe, Lorenzo understood she wasn't abandoning Lorenzo's father. She was embarking on a different season in her life, and his father's memory would always be cherished. The cassata was an extra bonus—a sharing of remarkable memories.

The oddest thing had happened when he came across The Pasta Junction's website. He saw the photo of the owner, Julie

Elliot, and he couldn't stop staring. Her blue eyes were enticing, yet mysterious, inspiring him to learn more about her. Her full red lips were pouty and curved. And, by the choice of her outfit and matching fedora, he realized she enjoyed film noir.

Exactly like him.

Before he phoned her, he'd double-checked to be certain she wasn't married, although gazing at her now, he wondered why she hadn't been scooped up years ago. What were all the single men in this town doing? Was the California sunshine making them blind?

Certainly he loved his grandmother and the marvelous memories they'd made together. Admittedly, though, he'd also used the recipe as a way to meet Julie in person, rather than simply booking the party on her website. Once they met, his decision became firm. He wanted to see her again, and couldn't wait until New Year's Day.

Okay, the poster had blatantly blared his interest, although he'd deemed it romantic when he purchased it. Now, for a man who earned his living by speaking into a camera to thousands of viewers, he found that expressing his feelings was surprisingly difficult.

"Lorenzo," she was saying, "there's a new movie playing at the Grover Theater. Or rather, I should say it's an old movie."

"Which one?"

"*The Big Sleep*."

"The movie starring Humphrey Bogart and Lauren Bacall?"

"The very same." Julie rewarded him with a wide grin.

"Private detective Philip Marlowe." Lorenzo paused. Did Julie hope he would ask her for a date? She was regarding him with anticipation in her eyes.

"Our finest film noir movie," she said.

Our film noir, because they shared a commonality. He

debated correcting her with a teasing *Our?*, but kept the question to himself. "I love the line from that movie, you know, the book shop scene," he said. "'You intrigue me.'"

"I believe Bogart used the word 'interest.'"

"'Interest me,'" Lorenzo corrected.

"Vaguely. Bogart said 'vaguely' at the end."

Lorenzo's gaze lingered on Julie's face. Yes, she certainly did interest him, and a whole lot more than vaguely.

Faintly, she smiled, as if reading his mind.

He cupped her chin, so she was forced to stare at him, and her smile warmed.

There were times when he wasn't certain how best to respond, and this became one of those moments. Should he kiss her?

She answered his silent question by drawing back. "Shall we try the cassata?" Her words tumbled out.

"Absolutely." He pushed back his stool and followed her lead.

"It may fall apart because it hasn't cooled long enough," she warned as he took her hand and led her to the cooktop.

Excellent. Then he'd have the excuse that it wasn't perfect, and he'd be able to see her again.

"We'll begin with a nibble." He hoped his grin flashed plenty of persuasion.

She pulled two dessert plates from a shelf, two forks and napkins, and sliced the cassata. She placed a portion on his plate and a second serving for herself.

He carried the plates to the counter as, with an apologetic murmur about hoping the coffee hadn't changed to mud yet, she poured them both more.

When they were once again perched on their stools, she bowed her head and recited a blessing. When the prayer ended, he murmured "Amen." Then he took a bite of the cassata.

As Julie predicted, the ricotta cheese separated from the still-steaming chocolate chips and fell to pieces.

He ignored her "I'm right" stare, shrugged, and forked another piece.

The cassata was good. Very good. The blending of chocolate and cheese melted in his mouth.

"Well?" she prompted.

He gestured to her plate. "You're the restaurant owner. What do you think?"

Slowly, she forked a sampling. "The combination is—"

She didn't finish and began coughing.

For an instant, he smiled, assuming she was elaborating her response with an exaggerated cough. Then her eyes widened.

He hesitated, then grasped her shoulders as his heart dropped. Surely she couldn't be choking on a small piece of cheesecake? She'd hardly eaten a bite. "Julie, can you speak?"

She didn't reply and continued coughing.

He slapped her across the back, attempting to dislodge any food stuck in her windpipe. With his other hand, which had begun to shake, he grabbed his cell phone, intending to call 911.

"Lorenzo—" Julie sputtered. "Don't. I'm okay."

His jaw clenched, and he grasped her forearm. "Are you certain?"

She nodded and dabbed at her watering eyes with the edge of her ruffled apron.

"I feared you ... you were smoking," he said.

"You mean choking."

"Right." He licked his lips, grabbed his bottle of water and drained it.

"I wasn't." She eyed his fingers clasped around her arm, the crumbs of cassata on her plate. "Okay, maybe I was. But I own a restaurant and have come to the rescue of many diners."

"What did you do?"

"Precisely what you did."

"So, in a way, I'm glad I was here, in case you needed medical assistance." His voice was still raspy with fright. He usually took charge during an emergency, but Julie in peril had had an odd effect on him. He'd almost been paralyzed for a frightening moment.

"In a way?" she asked.

"It's like in a movie. The hero saves the heroine in the end."

"Or vice versa."

His laugh nearly drowned out her next observation.

"This restaurant kitchen is hardly the setting for a crime drama," she pointed out.

Undeterred, he rummaged through the cabinets and found a glass. Filling it with water, he set it beside her. "Drink. Plus, I know why you choked."

Quickly, she drank. "Now you're a hard-boiled detective?"

"Only when it comes to cheesecake, which was too crumbly. Therefore ..." He watched her carefully as she chewed.

"Therefore?" she prompted.

"Therefore, you're clearly gifted." Inwardly, he congratulated himself on his adept subject change. He glanced at her hands, soft and delicate, as she grasped her fork. She accomplished so much with her hands, creating wonderful meals and, subsequently, memories.

"So, because I'm so gifted, we're all set?" She inclined her head in a slight nod and picked up her fork. "Can we agree the cassata is delicious?"

He directed a slow, meaningful gaze at the crumbs left on their plates. "Are you willing to bake another?"

She set her fork down. "Why?"

"Unfortunately, it's not as delicious as my grandmother's cassata." He affected a long sigh. "I suggest an extra cup of cherries and a half cup less of chocolate."

He should tell her the truth. But he couldn't. He'd already given her a poster declaring his feelings. They'd only just met, and he might come across as a love sick pudding-head. He'd done that once in his life and once was enough.

When she began to object, he said, "Therefore, can we meet again for another taste test?"

"Therefore?" She shook her head. "Lorenzo, these few days after Christmas were slow, but the restaurant is already booked for New Year's Eve and nearly full for the next few days."

He flashed a charismatic smile, hoping it so infectious she would immediately concur. "I can come by early tomorrow afternoon and assist you."

"Don't you work?"

"Morning meetings should be finished by noon. As long as I'm back at the station by four o'clock, I'm available."

"On Tuesday, we're only open for dinner."

He knew her restaurant's hours, but didn't want to confess he'd perused her website so often, he'd almost memorized it.

"Excellent. I'll pick up the ingredients beforehand." He smoothed out his grandmother's recipe and made a great show of producing a pen and paper from the pocket of his coat.

"I purchase most ingredients at a chef's food supply store," she said. "They're located on the other side of the bridge."

"I don't mind the extra distance. Didn't you mention the flavor might change depending on what factory produced the boxed cake mix? I'll stop by the grocer's in town."

"The corner grocer is not a factory, nor a chef's store," she replied. "Plus, this grocer wouldn't be the same as the one your grandmother shopped in years ago, would it?"

"True." He scooped up the last bit of crumbs on his plate.

An hour later, after nonstop animated conversation, he reluctantly glanced at the clock on the wall and sighed. "I should get to the studio."

"I'll watch your weather report tonight."

"You won't be working?"

"I usually watch it on the station's website."

His delighted gaze met hers. "Since when?"

"Since you became Bloomingfield's premier meteorologist." The tip of her tongue moistened her lips. Captivating him.

He cleared his throat. "Don't forget my gift."

Her gaze drifted to the poster and then to him. By her softened expression, she apparently knew why he'd selected that particular poster, and their love for film noir was only part of the reason. The real reason was the words.

He was falling for her. And he hoped that whenever she looked at the poster, she'd think of him.

"Shall we say twelve o'clock?" he asked.

She nodded. "Thank you for thinking of me, and for making my Christmas special." Her smile lit her entire beautiful face and twisted his insides upside down.

CHAPTER FIVE

The next morning, Julie spent a few hectic hours making pasta dough, receiving a food delivery, reviewing the accounts with her manager, and waiting for a pastry chef who never showed for his interview. With nothing more to do before Lorenzo arrived, Julie walked back to her third-floor apartment. The apartment was located on a tree-lined neighborhood only two blocks away from the restaurant.

Spurred by Lorenzo's invitation to fly to Italy with him, she'd done something the night before she rarely did. She'd surfed the internet, most notably the town of Calitri in Italy.

She wasn't stalking him, she told herself, she was researching Italy. The vivid descriptions of castle ruins and ancient cathedrals opened a realm of possibilities she hadn't considered before.

When she retired to her apartment, she entered her cheerful kitchen, painted a bright yellow, and brewed a mug of peppermint tea. She carried the mug into the living room, which she'd decorated in calming shades of green. French doors offered a panoramic view of Bloomingfield and opened onto an outdoor balcony with a wrought-iron railing. On sunny days, the room flooded with natural light, and on cool, rainy evenings, the wood-burning fireplace provided cozy warmth.

The previous evening, she'd rolled Lorenzo's poster out on the coffee table, anchoring it with books. Now as she stood in the living room, she deliberated on where to hang it.

"For what it's worth," she said aloud, "the poster is beautiful."

Once more reflecting on the words, she fastened it to a plain wall by the fireplace.

Taking her tea over to the couch, she phoned Sally at Bloomingfield Chocolate Shop. The shop was extremely popular and boasted a steady stream of devoted patrons. At a recent candy-making contest held in a local women's shelter, the shop's chocolate coffee fudge was voted first place. Since then, business had doubled.

"Are you busy?" Julie inquired when Sally answered the phone. "I know that's a silly question, considering how conscientious you are."

"Conscientious is overrated." Sally chuckled. Despite the trying work hours, the mischievous giggle of Sally's youth was still there.

As a tangle-haired imp, Sally had constantly teased Julie when they were children. Once they'd reached their teens, they'd become fast friends, and their conversations often lasted for hours. A few years younger than Julie, Sally's curly hair gave her a pixie look, while Julie preferred to style her hair in classic buns and pin curls.

"Overrated?" Julie repeated. "Being conscientious is how you get things done."

"Unfortunately, or fortunately, however you want to view it, our jobs, including Katie's as a lawyer, are demanding,"

Sally confirmed. "Even Ben. He's at the cash register cashing out customers. I'll wave to him for you."

Julie suppressed the urge to playfully inquire if Ben had ventured into the shop's kitchen, for he knew nothing about the candy-making process. Their older brother was a silent partner, but he often stepped into the chocolate shop to help.

"I'm sorting red bento boxes," Sally continued. "Believe it or not, I'm already planning Valentine's Day, a popular chocolate day in my candy part of town."

Julie chuckled. "Well, in my restaurant part of town, I'm managing the overbooked reservations for the New Year's holiday."

"Sounds like you had a profitable Christmas. You mentioned people waited in line for a table."

"Thankfully, we were able to accommodate every patient diner," Julie replied. "Although that's not the problem."

"There's a problem?"

Julie set her cell phone to speaker, placing it beside her, and picked up her mug of tea. "Yes, and it's Lorenzo Rossi."

After a thoughtful silence, Sally asked, "The good-looking meteorologist on the evening news?"

"He booked a first anniversary party for his mother and step-father at The Pasta Junction for New Year's Day."

"Gosh, that man is dazzling."

"Gosh? Dazzling?" Sally's statement earned a giggle from Julie. "You're not helping."

"Explain, please."

"I met with him yesterday. And I'm seeing him again today."

"Why? Is he pulling out of the booking and, for some odd reason, chooses to tell you in person?" Sally asked. "I guarantee you'll fill his table quickly."

"No, he's not canceling. Actually, it's just the opposite. Lorenzo is obsessed with his Italian grandmother's cheesecake recipe and wants to serve it at the party." A warm tingling coursed through Julie's body as she remembered sharing the cheesecake with him. She shook it off. "Can I also say that he is completely impossible?"

"We both encounter difficult customers. We're used to it."

After Julie's brief explanation regarding the taste testing, Sally's musical laugh erupted. "Why didn't you explain sooner? He's not interested in the cassata. He's interested in you."

"We just met."

"Love at first sight. It happens all the time, although I've never experienced anything of the sort."

Julie refrained from commenting. Her sister had endured a painful divorce and was now happily raising Clarissa, her beautiful daughter, as a single mother. Julie loved spending time with the little girl and taking her for sweets at the local ice cream parlor, which always earned her a cuddle and a "You're the best, Aunt Julie."

Julie glanced at the poster. "We're talking about Lorenzo Rossi."

"That's what I said. Love at first sight."

Shaking her head, Julie picked up her cell phone and stepped to the poster, and the eye-catching portrayal of a mysterious, beautiful woman. She'd read that the noir films of the 1940s had reflected the world weariness of the era after the war. Cool, businesslike heroines and nonchalant heroes, along with subdued lighting, embodied the sense of uncertain times. As she viewed the poster, her stomach tensed. Had she become an emotionless, efficient adult like the insouciant woman in the poster, thrusting all her energy into work and no longer taking precious opportunities to genuinely appreciate life?

"Hey?" Sally inquired. "Are you still there?"

"Yes, I'm here. I'm starting to suspect that any cassata I

bake for him will not be satisfactory," Julie said in a hushed voice.

And was that a bad thing? Then she'd get to see Lorenzo again.

She blinked. Is that what Lorenzo had intended all along?

"When will you meet him next?" Sally asked.

Julie peered at her watch. "In about an hour. He wants another taste test."

"Uh-huh. Because he wants to see you again." Sally voiced Julie's contemplations aloud. "And I can see through the phone that you're blushing."

"I'm not," Julie refuted, although her heated cheeks contradicted her.

"I bet you are," Sally said. "You always blush when you're attracted to a guy."

It went without saying that Sally was alluding to the time when Julie had been charmed by the married man. She'd gushed nonstop about him for weeks. That is, until she'd learned the truth.

Beyond a doubt, Lorenzo was different. The warmth in his eyes when they'd chatted about the scene from the movie *The Big Sleep*, the determination in his deep voice when he decided to phone the television station to inform them he'd be late, assured Julie he was sincere.

"I wonder if I should continue to meet with him alone at my restaurant," she said aloud. "It's not professional."

"You're being ridiculous," Sally scolded. "He isn't married, is he?"

"No."

"Divorced?"

"Not that I'm aware." Julie tried to suppress the images of the supermodels Lorenzo probably dated and chided herself for speculating. Based on his exceptional looks and charisma, she could only imagine. "But I haven't asked him."

"Does he know anything about your dating past?"

"I don't have a dating past."

"Then push your concerns aside and enjoy his gorgeousness." Sally paused. "Hang on. All the customers have left and Ben is quizzically watching me. I'll tell him I'm talking to you."

Sally cupped the phone. After several seconds of muted conversation, she laughed.

"I'm back," Sally said a moment later. "Ben spouted the funniest joke about a weatherman."

Julie shook her head in disbelief. "You told him about Lorenzo in under a minute?"

"Affirmative. What are siblings for, except to cheer each other on? Do you want to hear Ben's joke?"

"Do I have a choice?"

"Not really," Sally said. "So why was the old meteorologist worried?"

"I'm supposed to ask why, correct?"

"Of course."

Julie blew out a breath. "Why?"

"Because he was fearful the new weatherman would steal his thunder. Get it? Thunder?"

Julie chuckled. "I'll try to remember to pass along the joke to Lorenzo."

"Good. One more thing. Julie?"

"Yes?"

"I can't judge from watching Lorenzo on television if his persona is the real deal or not, but he comes across as a good guy. He seems genuine."

And he likes film noir, Julie thought. And black coffee. He also reacted quickly when he was afraid I was choking ...

"I feared you ... you were smoking."

"You mean choking."

His ashen face appeared in her mind as he'd mixed up his

words. His brilliant blue eyes had been overly bright. He'd been honestly concerned about her.

She sought to tear herself away from her reflections, yet she daydreamed about him. His slow easy smile, his tender kiss. Softly, she smoothed her fingers over her lips, remembering.

"Hello, Julie? Did I lose you again?" Sally asked.

She must stop thinking about him. "I'm here. Thank Ben for the joke."

"He's delighted to tell more whenever asked."

"Then we need to be certain we never ask." Despite herself, Julie giggled. "I love you both and we'll talk soon."

"We love you too. Oh, and Julie, Ben and I and Katie look forward to meeting your guy."

"He's not my guy, Sally."

"You're smitten. Admit it. Bring him into the chocolate shop."

Murmuring an agreement she assumed would never happen, Julie clicked off and studied the poster.

A beautiful woman has strolled into my peaceful life.

The words were a mirror of her own thoughts, although she reversed them.

A handsome man has strolled into my peaceful life.

CHAPTER SIX

*L*orenzo walked into Julie's restaurant at precisely one o'clock.

Elated anticipation had grown inside him all morning. The cassata excuse, which he'd originally intended as a means to get to know her better, was the highlight of his day. He'd spent his waking hours remembering each of their moments together and speculated on when he could introduce Julie to his family.

Certainly there was no better opportunity than New Year's Day, when everyone was present and he could introduce her as his ...?

His what? Date? Girlfriend? Perhaps more.

Perhaps less. They'd only just met, and relationships took stages to mature as people learned more about each other.

Nevertheless, with inborn optimism, he smiled. The promise of a delightful afternoon with Julie beckoned.

After he knocked on The Pasta Junction's green wooden door, she'd called out to him to come inside. "The door's unlocked," she added.

"I bought the ingredients at the corner grocer's." He

strode into the dining room and they acknowledged each other with cheerful greetings.

He followed her into the kitchen.

He set down the brown grocery bag, removed his beat-up leather jacket, damp from the rain, and draped it over a stool.

With a sigh, she busied herself with tidying cutlery.

"Anything the matter?" he asked with a smile. He hoped the smile hid his concern. She looked pale and tired. Although her resilience amazed him, her work responsibility was a challenging burden to carry on her own.

"A headache is coming on, and I realize it's stress because of the holiday season." She rubbed her temples, then her tight shoulders. "I'm grateful for my patrons, but also hoping my life calms down after the first of the year."

"Will it? Calm down?"

Uncertainly, she gazed at him. "Maybe."

"Some of those choices are up to you." He reached into the grocery bag and placed the cake mix, ricotta cheese, chocolate chips, and maraschino cherries on the counter. "I presume this is the correct boxed mix. It looks the same as the one I remember from my grandmother's house."

She quirked a delicate eyebrow. "How long is it since you baked a cassata?"

"Well, I'm thirty-two, and spent many afternoons with her throughout my childhood." He perused the label on the box. "Thus, over twenty years ago."

"It's highly doubtful the packaging stayed the same." Julie grinned, went to the cooler and brought back two bottles of water. He stepped aside as she poured the water into glasses.

He'd phoned her from the store to ask what type of ricotta he should purchase—low fat, fat free, or regular—and she'd instructed that regular ricotta was fine, and then remarked that the restaurant's coffee machine had broken down. She expected it would be repaired before the dinner crowd arrived and was concerned the fix might be costly. Still, she'd explained, a repair was better than purchasing a brand new machine.

As she started pulling out bowls and a wooden spoon, he couldn't stop admiring her. Her tight black denims, topped with a red holiday sweater, enhanced her slim curves. He gave her an appreciative appraisal from the tips of her blond hair, which was clipped into a side bun by a shiny gold barrette, to her sensible work shoes.

When she turned and picked up her water glass, he clinked his glass with hers. "Good afternoon, gorgeous."

Her shoulders relaxed. "Good afternoon, Lorenzo." She set down her glass and considered him. "I guessed you were younger than thirty-two years old."

"Thank you. I'm assuming you're complimenting me." He viewed her smooth complexion, the light sprinkling of freckles on the bridge of her nose, her glossy red lipstick. "May I ask how old you are?"

"Let's just say somewhere in my thirties. Not all women reveal their ages and I'm one of those women."

"I'm intrigued by a woman with a hint of mystery."

She batted her long dark eyelashes and laughed out loud. He laughed with her.

She was enchanting.

What if he arranged a trip to Italy and persuaded her to travel with him? He pictured them together in his beloved Calitri, wandering the narrow streets, while he translated Italian words and phrases and showed her his ancestral home nestled in the olive groves.

She touched her mouth, and he had the urge to step forward and kiss her. Instead, he set down his glass and embraced her. The feel of her warm, delicate body against his unexpectedly shook him.

. . .

*T*wo hours later, the cassata had been baked and was cooling. During the preparation, he'd hummed a venerable Italian melody, "O Sole Mio," theatrically flinging out his arms while he belted out the chorus, first in Italian, again in English.

Afterward, they sat at the counter, talking and laughing. Between mixing the ricotta and chopping maraschino cherries, she'd folded countless white napkins and polished the silverware to a gleaming finish. Today, the restaurant was only open for dinner beginning at six o'clock, she informed him, but he already knew that.

Soon afterward, she declared that she needed to make her trademark pasta for dinner.

"I can watch, can't I?" Lorenzo asked.

"Nope."

He grimaced. "Is pasta making some kind of trademark secret? Can't I even take notes?"

"No watching or taking notes." At his inquiring protest, she flashed a dazzling smile. "You can do better, because you can help me." She moved to a cabinet and brandished a frilly red apron.

"I like you a lot," he said. *Okay, more than a lot.* "But under no condition am I wearing an apron."

She drew out a white apron and tied it around herself. "See? Now we match."

With a muffled laugh, she gestured to the empty kitchen. "No one else is here, and I'm not anticipating a television crew arriving to film your weather report. Are you?"

He noted she was correct. With a sigh, he stood and held up his arms as she tied the red apron around his waist. He tucked the ends into the waistband of his jeans.

"Ideal," she teased when he twirled for her approval. "I admire a man who doesn't object to working in the kitchen."

"For you, I'll do anything." He stepped within inches of her and slid an arm around her waist. Gently, he swept a pin curl from her cheek. "And I do mean anything."

She turned, smiling up at him as her gaze warmed.

He felt happier than he'd been in a long time, and the reason stood clearly in his arms.

Julie was tall and slim, near his height, and a single word appeared in his mind as he gazed at her.

Knockout. Julie Elliott was a knockout.

She swung from him and he followed her to an open area in the rear room. There, she dragged out a large piece of stainless steel equipment.

"This is how I make fresh pasta," she said, "and this is a pasta machine."

Boy, was she ever proficient.

"How many pounds of pasta do you produce in a day?" he inquired.

"Five to six." She took out a bowl of dough from a cooler, placed a substantial amount on the flat counter, and began kneading. "Truly, there is a distinguishable taste difference between dry pasta and fresh," she said.

"What are the ingredients for your dough?" He brought out his cell phone and snapped a picture of her. "For me," he assured at her distracted expression.

The photo on her website depicted a playful, yet sultry, Julie. This photo, Julie preparing her beloved pasta, was the real Julie, the working Julie.

Although, wasn't she a combination of both women? Didn't everyone have multiple characteristics, multiple selves?

"Eggs, flour, olive oil, and kosher salt," she was saying. "I made the dough earlier, covered it with plastic wrap and let it rest. Today is a happy day because you're here to help."

"A happy day and a happy man who is happy to oblige," he quipped as he put away his cell phone. "What comes next?"

"Let's wash our hands. After we dry them thoroughly, we'll dust them with flour."

After their hands were clean and white with flour, they doubled back to the counter. "First, I flatten the dough." She wielded her rolling pin. "Next I roll it."

"Fascinating."

"And this is where you come in."

He stiffened. "Me?"

She fitted the pasta machine to the counter and adjusted the clamp, demonstrating that it kept the machine steady. "Keep adjusting the knob until the dough becomes thin."

He worked cautiously at first, turning the crank with one hand while feeding dough into the machine with the other. After more than a dozen tries and several sheets of ruined pasta, he began turning out expertly thin sheets.

"Your dough is pliable," he remarked. "If I weren't so diligent, I'd applaud your talents, but I can't let go of the crank."

"Applause is always appreciated," she laughed, and bobbed her head toward the pasta machine. "Don't forget to keep dusting the dough with flour, or else it will stick."

"You're being bossy."

"That's because I'm the boss."

He chuckled, shaking his head at the discarded pasta. "I'm guessing your noodles are amazing, and that you're thrilled I don't actually work here."

"Similar to any art, pasta making takes time and patience. You're doing splendid." She paused. "I forgot you've never eaten here."

"That will change," he assured her. "Because we're a couple."

Her lips parted. "We're a couple?"

He was intensely aware of his own heartbeat. "That is, if you agree."

"I'm tied up countless hours every day." Ruefully, she shook her head and placed her hand over his. The tender gesture caused his thoughts to whirl.

"Is that a yes or a no?" he asked.

"It's a cautious ... yes."

"Good," he replied. "We'll make it work."

She made an impressive show of delight by displaying a wide grin, and any frustration at his failed pasta attempts, or whether she reciprocated his feelings, quickly evaporated. Already, she was filling his days with enchantment.

"My 'famous,'" she finger quoted, "fettuccini uses the same dough. For lasagna, I would double the recipe." She quickly sliced his long pasta sheets into smaller sheets of equal length. "This pasta will boil in under a minute."

"But it takes a substantial number of hours to make, not to mention the daily commitment," he said. He finished cranking the last portion of the dough. Then he floured sheet pans as she instructed, laying out the strips to dry.

"Once you start making fresh, it's tough to reintroduce dried," she remarked. "Fresh pasta tastes silkier and creamier."

"Plus, you're saving money."

"Perhaps. But when you factor in the cost of this machine and my labor ..." She set down the rolling pin. "Then not so much."

"Are you strapped financially?" he asked.

"Money is always tight."

He avoided eye contact with her. He knew from firsthand experience the expense of investing in a restaurant and subsequently losing it when the restaurant shuttered. Ironically, he could even recite the statistics. Sixty percent of restaurants failed, even if they were excellent.

She nodded toward the main kitchen. "Ready to try the cassata?"

"Absolutely."

After all that cranking, he was starving. Welcoming scents of chocolate and cherries greeted him as they stepped into the kitchen. He remembered where she kept the dishes and forks and brought them to the counter.

She plated their servings. As she'd done the previous day, she bent her head and murmured a quiet blessing, and he followed her lead.

Then he savored a bite of cassata. The texture was heavenly, the sweetness of the cherries blending seamlessly with the chocolate.

"Well?" She scooped up another bite. "I assume you're satisfied, because this is delicious."

His first instinct was to take her in his arms and declare that in order to be satisfied, he needed to see her again.

He thought quickly and didn't rely on his instincts. Yes, they were now "a couple," but their bond was still fragile. After his hurtful relationship with a cheater who had ultimately betrayed him, he'd vowed never to fall in love again. Casual dating? Certainly, and with more women than he cared to count. Anything more? Absolutely not.

And yet, in merely a few days he'd fallen for a sharp-witted, ambitious beauty who softened his heart with her contagious smile.

So here he stood, confronting a dilemma. If he admitted the cassata was perfect, he wouldn't see Julie again until he was a customer at her restaurant, surrounded by his family. She was too busy to actually date him until after the holidays.

"It's good," he replied hesitantly. "However ..."

She subjected him to a narrowed gaze. "Is that the only word in your vocabulary when it comes to describing this cassata?"

He untied his frilly apron and draped it over a chair, taking his time to formulate his reply. "As you instructed, I bought whole milk ricotta for this recipe. However, I just remembered my mother specifically told me she is watching her waistline."

"You just remembered?"

He shifted and shrugged on his jacket. "Therefore, let's try the recipe with low-fat ricotta."

"You're the person who bought the ingredients."

"Remember? I forgot."

"Convenient," she countered. "May I point out that your Italian buffet will consist of hundreds of calories between the pasta, garlic bread, and meatballs?"

"Still, I'd like to test the recipe using low-fat ricotta," he said. "In addition, this time you should measure the quantities exactly. Level off the cinnamon and cocoa in the measuring cup."

She plunked her hands on her hips. "*Therefore,* you're suggesting I measure exact amounts of ingredients which aren't listed?"

He grinned. "Something like that."

"Lorenzo, you can't rely on math for baking or cooking, because the process is creative and subjective." Her spine stiffened. "And I prefer to do things my way."

He strode to her and tipped up her chin. "One more taste test?"

"Why?"

"Because I want to see you again," he said softly. He cuddled her close for a lengthy, thorough kiss.

When he lifted his head, her soft blue eyes gazed up at him. "I'd like to see you too."

His attention was diverted by his buzzing cell phone. He reviewed the message flashing across his screen, and an idea took hold.

"Tonight there is a meteor shower that should turn into an outburst," he said.

She stepped away from him and tugged off her apron. "I have no idea what you're talking about."

"The meteor shower comes from the constellation Ursa Major," he explained. "Most people recognize it as the Big Dipper, although it's technically not a constellation."

He studied her blank smile, her tentative nod.

"Do you know what a constellation is?"

"Naturally," she replied. "A chance grouping of stars, although you're clearly better versed on the subject than I am."

"That's because I'm a meteorologist, constantly studying weather patterns and the sky. Astronomy has a noteworthy effect on climate."

Her eyes sparkled. "I find astronomy fascinating."

"Excellent. Now we share another commonality." He opened the Star Tracker app on his phone and cited the stars blanketed by a black sky. "Are you interested in seeing meteors tonight?"

She hesitated. "I'm interested, sure. But—"

"A group of amateur astronomers meets twice a month at a field behind Bloomingfield High School. They're called the Stargazers. Ever hear of them?"

She accompanied him to the door. "No."

"The high school field is ideal for star watching, because the mountains block the city lights. Oftentimes, the Stargazers are there."

"Perhaps some other time." She sighed. "Tonight is a busy night at the restaurant."

"You can't work constantly, Julie. Besides, sky conditions are ideal." Desperately, he tried to keep his features straight, because he recognized her interest by her intent gaze. "I'll even bring my telescope."

She shook her head. "Impossible. Maybe after the holidays …" At her head shake, blond wisps broke free from her bun and fell across her cheek. "The restaurant can't operate without me."

"I'll pick you up after work at ten o'clock. Better yet, I'll come earlier." He deliberately ignored her observation about being indispensable. Once, he'd harbored the same mindset and had discovered a surprising awakening. The Pasta Junction could indeed function without her for a few hours, just as another weatherman had neatly and quickly filled Lorenzo's weatherman position in Atlanta.

Tenderly, he kissed her cheek. "This event only happens every twenty-four years. You don't want to miss it."

"I can't commit. After the restaurant closes, there's clean-up—"

"I'll help you. The best viewing for the meteor shower is around eleven o'clock until midnight. Thus you won't be out long, and I promise to deliver you home safely."

She glanced at his phone. "I've never allowed myself the time to study the stars."

"They're predicting hundreds of meteors. The outburst will last about fifteen minutes and promises an extraordinary show." He paused, then reminded, "Once every twenty-four years..."

"You are very persuasive." She granted him a flirtatious smile, presenting such a charming image he was torn between kissing her again or the correspondingly pleasant prospect of feasting his gaze on her.

"You were the expert when it came to pasta making. Although truth be told," he reminded, "you were a little bossy."

She shot a quick gaze toward the ceiling. "I was not because—" She broke off and frowned. "Was I?"

"A tad." He chuckled. "Anyway, tonight is an opportunity for me to demonstrate my knowledge."

"All these exciting adventures," she murmured. "You bring the charming Italian man charisma thing to a whole new level."

"If I can persuade you to come with me, then I'm doing my job." He pocketed his phone and kissed her temple. "I'll pack a blanket and thermos of coffee."

"I'd honestly love to go." She wavered. "Should I bring food? I invariably have leftovers."

"Does your restaurant have a takeout or delivery service?"

"No," she replied. "I'm missing out on a profitable opportunity, right?"

"A service would provide a positive monthly addition to your income."

"I may try your recommendation. Mr. Rossi, you're a wizard."

"Hardly." He laughed, then sobered. "Where does the excess restaurant food end up?"

"I donate everything to a soup kitchen in town."

"Do you usually have pasta leftovers?"

"More often than not."

"Wow, I'll finally get to taste the pasta I toiled over." He lifted stray strands of her hair and nuzzled her neck, her chin, her lips.

"The pasta you toiled over for all of thirty minutes," she joked.

"With my knowledge and your expertise ..." he murmured, changing a line from a film he suspected she knew.

"We might go places," she finished, instantly proving that she did. "Although you're misquoting Frank Chambers from *The Postman Always Rings Twice*."

"Did you know the movie was made in 1946?"

"I did. And I loved every minute of it."

And I love you.

The revelation startled him. Obviously, he couldn't be in love with her. Their shared experiences had just begun. Plus they were on completely different tracks. She was immersed in her work while he'd learned to slow down and enjoy life. She was a true workaholic, and sometimes that got tiresome. Lately, it seemed everyone he knew was on the job 24/7. The way of the world, he supposed.

Stop analyzing, he ordered himself. They were simply *a couple*.

"Has anyone ever refused you?" She opened the front door to the rush of a warm breeze. The rain had stopped. Energetic sounds drifted from the street—the clink of coffee cups from people sitting outside at the nearby café, the whisper of tree branches, pedestrians chatting as they wandered in and out of the bookstore.

An occasional car was the only traffic. The restaurant's historic building was positioned in an ideal location, exuding traditional appeal in an intimate neighborhood.

"I don't remember." He gave a quiet chuckle. "Furthermore, I'll never refuse any of your requests, so we're even."

"That's encouraging." Her lilting laughter lit her entire face.

He laughed, enjoying the exhilaration of relishing every available second with this extraordinary woman.

CHAPTER SEVEN

*S*tar gazing. She'd actually gone star gazing.

Julie flopped on her living room couch and went over the previous evening in her mind.

True to his word, Lorenzo had arrived at The Pasta Junction well before ten o'clock. He'd worn his usual jeans, weathered chukka boots and scruffy leather jacket. Upon seeing her, he greeted her with a kiss. His chiseled features were all male, and her pulse leaped at the sound of his rich voice, his enthusiastic, "Hello, gorgeous."

Immediately, he went to work wherever she directed, assisting the bus boys and waiters and waitresses with an agreeable smile while they exchanged pleased looks with one another.

The restaurant's vibe was different from the quiet space he'd seen the last two days, he informed Julie. Now it purred with efficiency, as all the employees got down to the issue of cleanup.

She and Lorenzo decided to dine inside the restaurant, sliding into a booth in the formal dining area. The adjoining lounge featured a bar and large-screen television. Idly, they followed the news while enjoying a hasty meal of homemade fettuccini and crusty Italian bread.

"Delicious," Lorenzo pronounced, lifting his gaze now and then to the wall clock before focusing on the bowl, heaped with pasta, in the center of the table.

"Enjoy another helping," Julie encouraged.

"It's getting late." Reluctantly, he pushed back his chair. "I'm torn between eating more or stargazing, but we don't want to miss the meteor shower."

"The heavens won't wait for pasta?"

He exhaled. "Unfortunately not."

"Well then, return here tomorrow. I guarantee there will be more pasta."

"Are you extending an invitation?"

"You bet." She tugged off her apron and declared that she ought to freshen up. He immediately stood to stack their dinner plates and carry them to the kitchen. When she circled back, his slow, appreciative grin filled her with pleasure.

In the restroom, she brushed her hair until it snapped, leaving it loose and spilling over her shoulders. When she gazed in the mirror to apply a touch of red lipstick, she smiled at her reflection. Despite the many hours on her feet, her smile was genuine, and her complexion positively glowed.

"You are gorgeous," he said when she returned to the dining area. He brought a tender smile to his intent gaze. "And I like when you wear your hair down."

There was no denying that her pulse tingled every time he complimented her.

"Thanks." With a last fluff of her hair, she added water bottles to his backpack while he shrugged on his jacket. While the day's temperatures had been comfortable, a night in a large, open field would be chilly, and she donned a coral suede coat for extra warmth.

When they reached the open field, he set up two folding chairs, a tray table, a blanket on the ground, and then adjusted his telescope. Inky blackness enveloped them, and even though Lorenzo stood near, his figure blurred.

"Conditions are ideal for star gazing," he explained. "No rain is in the forecast and the sky is clear and not hazy."

She peered around. "Is this a good viewing spot?"

"Excellent. I'm here often. A while back, I instructed the astronomer's club on the various constellations."

Absently listening while he described why the best time to go star gazing was when the moon wasn't visible because moonlight washed out fainter stars, she dug into his backpack, poured two cups of coffee into cups and set them on the table.

He always remembered everything. In addition, he displayed gentlemanly characteristics she appreciated—holding doors open for her, standing when she stood, and complete absorption in her words whenever she spoke. Already, she was appreciating his insight and wisdom when she described a problem at the restaurant and he came up with a thoughtful solution.

Bighearted yet humble, he'd mentioned he volunteered weekly at a national park close by and cleaned up litter.

He loved nature. And because he was a meteorologist, a scientist who studied weather, he was also a perfectionist. She welcomed perfection, though food and creativity were her strong suits.

"Do you recognize the constellations?" he asked as he clicked his coffee cup against hers with a smile and a toast.

"Raise your cup to the extraordinary night sky," he said.

And she did. Here on this field, exuding enthusiasm and exuberance, he created a celebratory event.

She sipped her coffee and set down her cup. "A little."

"Where's Gemini?" He gestured upward, and a slight breeze caught his question. "You can see the constellation with your naked eye."

She shivered. "Perhaps if I knew where to look."

He glided his arm around her, and murmured, "There."

She leaned against his muscled chest and fixated on the pitch-black sky and brilliant pricks of stars, following his forefinger as he connected the stars with an imaginary line forming recognizable stick figures.

Together, they sat on the woolen blanket, and he suggested she lie back and peer upward. "The horizon will be at the edge of your peripheral vision," he said, "and the sky will fill everything you see."

She did as he directed, lying beside him on the woolen blanket. He waited until her eyes adjusted to the dark, then pointed out each star of the Little Dipper. Meteors streaking through the sky immediately captured her attention.

In awe was the only term she could use to describe the next fifteen minutes. The meteors' tiny sizes and penetrating brilliance, along with Lorenzo's throaty laugh as she excitedly gasped whenever she identified one, prompted her to forget everything except the extraordinary thrill of the moment.

"This entire evening is magical," she said.

He pulled her tight and cupped her face in his hands. "You're magical."

Her heart beat so hard and fast in her chest, she thought surely he must hear it.

When the meteor shower ended, she fully faced him. "What is the difference between a shooting star and a falling star?"

"They are the same," he replied. "Meteors travel at tens of thousands miles per hour and burn because of the powerful atmospheric friction."

"Such a technical answer," she teased.

He smiled. "Occasionally you'll be lucky enough to witness a meteor plunge to earth. Thus, your falling star."

"Do you consider yourself a lucky man?" She gazed at his handsome face. Although the night was dark, she could discern the intense blueness of his eyes. Pausing, she surveyed his expression. "And why are you grinning like a Cheshire cat?"

"Because since I met you," he whispered, his face inches from hers, "I'm feeling fortunate and truly blessed."

Caught between joy and affection at his admission, she quietly stated, "So am I."

He shot her a gratified glance and skimmed his lips across her temple. "I intend to make you very, very happy."

Beneath a black velvet sky and twinkling stars, he drew her close and kissed her. His scent was the outdoors, mixed with a whiff of leather.

Close by, a chorus of high-pitched katydids serenaded them with their buzzing. He held her for a long while, his arms enfolding her.

Briefly, he closed his eyes, and she studied his features. His eyebrows were dark, his lashes thick and black and spiky. She shifted, and he gathered her closer. His response was unconscious, she assumed, but she was pleased with the idea that he wished her near.

It wasn't necessary, she dreamily reflected. She harbored no intention of drawing away, for she was falling in love with him. And she was surprised, because her love for him had developed so swiftly. When it came to her affections, she'd hidden behind a sturdy shield that had protected her. She'd been hurt once, and recovery took time.

But the moment had come to let down her shield, she decided, and she embraced the feelings of love and trust.

Lorenzo's second kiss was deeper, lengthier, and she

responded by laying her hand on his cheek and responding with desire and certainty. With him, she could hardly contain the emotions welling inside her. She knew this vital, intelligent man was quickly winning a permanent place in her heart.

After their hour together had drifted to two, they packed their things and prepared to leave. Several people waved and shouted greetings as they started for Lorenzo's car.

"The amateur astronomers I mentioned," he murmured. "I assumed they were somewhere in this field tonight." He returned their waves and grinned.

"Lorenzo, what is your reaction to tonight's meteor display?" a stocky fellow called out. He wore binoculars around his neck and carried a telescope.

"I'm humbled by the universe," Lorenzo responded.

"Will we hear about the meteors on tomorrow's evening news?"

"Possibly, if my managers give me the go-ahead."

"Will you speak at one of our meetings again?" someone else asked. "You were sensational in October. Our members are still discussing the information you presented."

"I'm glad to oblige," Lorenzo replied.

"Your girlfriend is lovely," an older woman said.

Julie gazed up at him. Without question, he was a favored television personality among the townspeople of Bloomingfield, and their regard for him seemed to cautiously embrace her too.

With his arm securely around her, Lorenzo agreed with the woman, then tipped up Julie's chin.

"You can't kiss me in front of the entire astronomer's club," she whispered, knowing her face heated and feeling eternally grateful for the darkness.

"With your permission I can." He waited a beat. "Permission granted?"

Seeing his affectionate gaze, she smiled. "No one can refuse your Italian—"

"Charm," he finished with a mischievous gleam. He bent his head and soundly kissed her.

Somewhere in the distance, a cheer rose up. In response, Lorenzo locked her in a tight embrace and kissed her again.

CHAPTER EIGHT

*a*s the following days merged into a frenzy of activity, New Year's Eve arrived.

Julie stood in the foyer of The Pasta Junction and cradled her cell phone to her ear.

"I need your help," she told Sally while she hung a broad white sign with black lettering on the front door.

"'I was thinking about that dame upstairs.'" Julie quoted the sign aloud.

"Huh?" Sally asked.

"I'm citing Fred MacMurray's words in *Double Indemnity*. Anyone familiar with film noir will recognize the famous line immediately."

"I've never watched those movies," Sally said.

"Once you start, you'll be hooked." Julie circled her attention to the never-ending business at hand—organizing and preparing an outstanding gala. Three days earlier, on the spur of the moment, she'd decided to offer a glamorous, film noir theme. She posted the event on her website, inviting women to wear sleek gowns, elegant gloves and saucy hats. *Dress up or dress down*, she wrote. *All are welcome*.

She listed three-piece pin-striped suits as an option for men.

"So you require my help because …?" Sally reverted their conversation back to the reason Julie had phoned. As usual, Sally was ringing out customers in her chocolate shop, and the simultaneous chime of the cash register and chatting people brought a smile to Julie's face. Ben and his girlfriend, Maise, had taken Clarissa, Sally's daughter, to an afternoon matinee.

Katie, their lawyer sister, as Ben teasingly called her, was out of town for the holidays and vacationing in Colorado.

"I need your help because you're the chocolate expert, Sally," Julie replied. She stepped back to peruse the dining room. For late-night munchies, she'd serve popcorn in striped containers, arrayed on black linen tablecloths. Beverages included festive bubbly cocktails, both alcoholic and nonalcoholic, and dinner would be served on gleaming white plates offset by black chargers. After a balloon drop and confetti at midnight, she'd added a one o'clock a.m. supper buffet, expecting her guests might be hungry again. She'd also partnered with a local cab company to offer free rides home to revelers after the festivities ended.

Easygoing background music, moody jazz arrangements featuring a saxophonist accompanied by a string quartet, enhanced the setting, and Lorenzo's poster hung prominently on one wall.

Lorenzo. She stared at the poster, recalling so many images of him.

His shoulders quaking with laughter at her exclamations upon seeing hundreds of meteors, the attractive white smile that flew across his face whenever he gazed at her, the stubborn way he crossed his arms when he declared yet another baking session was in order.

Since her flirtation with the married guy a few years ago,

she'd held every man at arm's length. Her emotions hadn't seemed alive.

But with Lorenzo ...Around him she melted. When they weren't together, she struggled to focus on her job. However, work didn't seem as important anymore. Perhaps she was suffering from burnout. More likely, she was deeply in love with a man she'd only met less than two weeks ago.

And the reality of the situation sent a heated pulse through her body.

"Hello?" Sally asked.

"Sorry."

"You do that a lot these days."

Julie flinched. "Do what?"

"Daydream, and it has something to do with a certain drop-dead gorgeous weatherman who'll be on TV at six o'clock tonight. You're still seeing him, correct?"

"Every day," Julie replied. "And I just wanted to tell someone that the last cassata he and I baked came out just as delectable as the previous two."

"Okay, good. So again, my help is needed because ..."

Julie spun on her heels for the kitchen, realizing her buffet table lacked champagne flutes. "Because *I* declared the cassata delicious."

"Then I think I know where this conversation is going." Sally laughed. "Somehow I get the impression that Lorenzo didn't share your enthusiasm?"

"Maybe I should add more chocolate chips to the recipe to appease him?" Julie stopped in mid step. "This time, he claimed there was something not quite right about the taste."

"Uh huh. Look, I'm a chocolate candy expert, not a baker. Pouring chocolate chips into a cheesecake isn't my forte."

"Get this." Julie peered at the evening menu and lost her train of thought. The Pasta Junction would serve a la carte dining from five until eight, and a toast from ten o'clock until the early morning buffet.

"Get what?" Sally prompted.

"Lorenzo claimed he suddenly realized that a first wedding anniversary is a paper anniversary," Julie said.

"Suddenly?"

"Yes. Therefore, he wants the cassata brought to his mother's anniversary table in a box."

"Like ... a cardboard box?"

"Cardboard, paper. He didn't say."

"I display my chocolate candy in bento boxes. What size is the cassata?"

"We're doubling the recipe. Thus, a sizable box is preferable."

"I'll look around and bring something tonight and leave it in your back office. Ben and I and Maise plan on dining at your restaurant around seven. Clarissa is coming too, obviously."

"Excellent. Don't forget the theme is black and white."

"My daughter and I are matchy-matchy. Black poodle skirts and starchy white blouses."

"You nailed it. Talk to you later."

*A*t first when Lorenzo walked into The Pasta Junction at ten o'clock that evening, Julie didn't see him. Instead she sensed his presence when heads swung toward the door. He had a tangible, confident personality that filled the room.

Clearing empty glasses on her path to the kitchen, she swiveled.

For a second he remained in the lobby, conversing with the maître d' who accepted his black leather jacket. All the while, Lorenzo's gaze skimmed the dining room. With a flush of excitement, she knew he searched for her.

Their gazes connected, and she set down the glasses.

Quickly, he fixed his dinner jacket on an empty chair, weaved around the candlelit tables and swept her into his arms for a kiss.

"You've outdone yourself tonight, Julie," he said. "The restaurant looks spectacular and you are ..." He stepped back, frankly admiring her glamorous V-neck black gown, slinky and flaring at the hem, with scalloped lace embellished sleeves. Tiny diamond earrings, strappy sandals and her trademark fedora hat completed the outfit. She'd brought her white faux fur coat and black opera gloves to wear later when Lorenzo drove her home.

She lifted an eyebrow at his loss for words. "I am ...?"

"Exquisite. A femme fatale."

Her breath caught at the gentleness in his voice. "Thank you."

She took in his powerful shoulders fitted in a snowy-white shirt, his narrow waist and long legs encased in black pants topped with black suspenders. Her heart did a flip, and she battled to keep her emotions in check. He'd dressed the part, emanating masculinity, and it was clear that every woman in the dining room had set down her fork to marvel at his exceptional looks.

"I hoped to arrive sooner," he said. "But the second my TV segment was over, the station held a staff party to celebrate the holiday ... All the while, 'I was thinking about that dame upstairs.'"

She chuckled, burying her escalating attraction behind a jest. "If you mean me, I'm not upstairs."

His gaze fixed intently on her. The buoyant mood grew serious. "Good. I like you near me."

She swallowed. "I'm thrilled you're here. We'll ring in the

new year together." She gestured to the packed dining room, the waiters traveling from table to table. "As you can see, it's one of the busiest nights of the year."

He grimaced. "Duly noted."

"Don't you like big crowds?"

"Not a bit," he softly replied.

"You're an extrovert, so I'm surprised to hear you say that."

Sharply, he glanced at her. "Why would you assume I'm an extrovert?"

"You're a public figure and on television every day where you're viewed by thousands."

"You're describing me in front of the camera in a closed-off area with people I know and trust, and where I'm comfortable." He reached for her hand and steered her into a quiet corner. "In truth, I'm an extroverted introvert."

"What does that mean? You're friendly and outgoing. You spoke at the astronomer's meeting."

"On television and in a setting I can control," he said. "Nonetheless, what people don't see is that I go home afterwards to recharge my batteries in solitude."

"Julie?" From a nearby table, a familiar woman's voice called out to them. "Aren't you going to introduce us?" Sally gaily waved, then attempted to pat her springy curls back into place. She'd declared years ago that no matter how many straightening products she used, in the end it was futile.

She and her daughter Clarissa displayed matching outfits, although Clarissa kept pulling at the collar of her starched blouse. Dark-haired Ben sported a suit and was smiling at his date, chestnut-haired and green-eyed Maise, who wore a broad-brimmed hat that dipped over one eye.

Julie shot Lorenzo a rueful glance. "My family wants to meet you."

There was a noticeable pause before he responded.

"Right." He picked up a non-alcoholic cocktail from a passing waiter, took a gulp, and kept a death grip on his glass. "Okay."

She felt his guard go up and couldn't understand why. He was so upbeat and witty. Why would he greet meeting her family with such unease, just because he was an introvert? They were merely four people, and one was a little girl.

She gave his hand a squeeze and led him over to them.

After introductions, Sally grabbed Lorenzo's arm and led him into the lounge to see the holiday decorations. Odd, yes, but Sally had been eager to talk with Lorenzo, and they were hardly gone a couple minutes.

When they returned, Ben merrily declared to Lorenzo that he had a stack of weatherman jokes, and inquired whether Lorenzo wanted to hear one. "Did you tell him my other joke?" he asked Julie.

"I'm sorry. I forgot."

"Well, this one is better." Ben angled toward Lorenzo.

"I can't wait," Lorenzo informed him. Still standing with Julie while the others sat, he set his drink on the table.

"A weatherman broke both of his arms and his legs," Ben began, "and he phoned the television station from the hospital. Guess what he told them?"

Laughing, Julie held up a hand. "The weatherman couldn't report to work because of his injuries?"

Ben grinned. "Nope. He informed the station about his four casts. Get it? Forecasts."

All three women, Julie, Maise, and Sally, dissolved into exaggerated laughter, and Clarissa giggled and clapped her hands. Her rosy red cheeks and sweet personality had brought abundant joy to the Elliot family, and Julie bent to hug her.

Lorenzo reached for his drink. "I get it, yes." He smiled,

although his smile didn't seem sincere. "Your joke is ... amusing."

"Have you heard that joke before?" Julie murmured to him as they walked away.

"About a thousand times," he replied.

After her family left, Lorenzo helped Julie wherever she asked, which was mostly keeping the patrons happy. In fact, he demonstrated a sixth sense regarding restaurant management, working out details with the staff before they became readily apparent.

All the while, she was absorbed in speculation. Although he'd acted personable with her family, he'd also seemed dismissive. When Sally had suggested they all get together soon, Lorenzo's posture had stiffened.

Okay, he was uncomfortable, an introvert, although no one would suspect by watching him. His smile remained in place, his manner relaxed and sociable.

She peered around. How could an enormous crowd, or an impromptu meeting with her family, not invigorate him?

The new year countdown began a short while later, and Lorenzo assisted Julie and the waitstaff in distributing leis and noisemakers to the guests.

"Oh no!" Julie grabbed a noisemaker, whirled, and brought a shaky hand to her forehead. "Where are the party hats? It's almost midnight!" She rushed to a side table and bent to search beneath the tablecloth for the feather tiaras and light-up fedoras. "I must have left them in the back room."

"You did, and I found them." Lorenzo edged her toward the waiters who were distributing the hats.

Amazed and touched to realize he'd taken care of another detail for her, she straightened and beamed into his handsome, smiling face.

When they'd first met, she'd been uneasy because she'd assumed he was married. Afterward, because he was so lethally good-looking and well-regarded, she'd been reluctant to admit her feelings. Now, as the clock was about to herald a new year, she had a strong urge to tell him how much she cared. But, she warned herself, she was perched dangerously close to the edge of a perilous cliff, and she'd already been hurt once in love.

She pushed aside her reservations and spoke aloud what she'd been thinking ever since he'd gifted her the poster. "A handsome man has strolled into my peaceful life."

He tipped up her chin. "And a beautiful woman has strolled into mine."

They angled toward the television screen in the lounge area. Along with a tide of revelers, they counted off the seconds until midnight.

"Ten, nine, eight, seven, six, five, four, three, two, one … Happy New Year!"

Lorenzo embraced her. On cue, the waiter in charge of the sound system put on "Auld Lang Syne," sung by a lone Scottish man. Tears pricked Julie's eyes.

Lorenzo held her close, swaying with the music.

"I've always loved that song," she whispered.

"And I love you," he said quietly.

Her gaze flew to his face. Wait, what? He said he loved her.

A tremble of excitement quickened her pulse. And yet she couldn't respond to his heartfelt declaration. It was too soon. Too soon to put herself out there and become vulnerable to …

To what?

Still, she didn't reply.

She stole a look at his shuttered expression before a waitress apologized for the interruption and declared they were out of popcorn.

Julie hightailed it into the kitchen to solve the minor crisis by substituting the popcorn with pretzels.

Lorenzo came up behind her. "I have an awesome idea." He wrapped his arms around her waist. "Let's take in a movie at the Grover Theater tonight."

She wheeled around. "The cinema is showing a movie tonight?"

"Yes, remember? One of the most popular film noir movies."

"*The Big Sleep?*"

Lorenzo grinned. "There's a showing at one. If we hurry, we'll make it."

"One o'clock in the morning? Who would go to a movie at that time?"

"We would."

"Lorenzo, I can't leave my staff to fend for themselves."

He perused the kitchen and half-dozen employees, the babble of cheery voices as they moved about their tasks preparing for the supper buffet. "They seem extremely efficient to me."

"I've never attended a movie at this time of night. Or day, depending on how you view it. Plus, I have an anniversary party to prepare for tomorrow."

"*My* party doesn't begin until three."

"Which is when my restaurant opens," she reminded. In addition, she planned to bake the cassata *without* his assistance. Intent on facilitating the early morning supper preparations, she attempted to scurry past him.

He braced his hands on either side of the door frame, blocking her way. "Tonight is special. It's New Year's Eve."

"The clock chimed midnight a half hour ago." Despite her protests, she knew she couldn't refuse him, and admitted as much. She dashed to the back office to retrieve her coat and gloves.

By the time she came back, he'd reclaimed his leather jacket.

He helped her on with her coat and extended his arm. "Ready?"

"You are impossible." She couldn't resist smoothing a lock of black hair from his forehead.

He smiled. "My SUV is parked a block away. Wait in the lobby. The weather is cold tonight."

"I can brave the cold."

"I'll pick you up. Wait here."

"Does anyone ever refuse you?" With a laugh in her voice, she placed her hand in the crook of his arm and walked with him to the lobby. A waft of wind teased her hair as he opened the door, and he gently swept the stray strands from her cheek.

Slowly, languorously, he appraised her. "Not on a marvelous night like this," he murmured, and sealed his statement with a kiss.

CHAPTER NINE

*N*ew Year's Eve with Lorenzo should have ended marvelously, the way Lorenzo had described it.

It didn't.

The following morning arrived prematurely for Julie, and she'd overslept. Still tired from the night before, she showered quickly and got dressed. As she paused at the French doors in her apartment and gazed out at a dazzlingly bright day, her thoughts veered to the previous evening.

After the movie had let out at three a.m., she and Lorenzo had strolled hand in hand toward his SUV, laughing and chatting. Save for the streetlights, the darkness was dense, the air cool. She looked around at her beloved hometown of Bloomingfield, the thick Ponderosa pines, the mountains soaring in the distance, and felt utter serenity. Soon, the sun would streak through the tree boughs in bright beams of daylight, and the mountain peaks would overshadow the horizon.

"What we're doing is called a *passeggiata* in Italy," Lorenzo said.

"Which means?"

"It's an Italian tradition, and everyone in the town participates. People dress up and take a leisurely stroll. Usually on Sunday evenings or a holiday."

"Today is a holiday," she said. "And I can grow accustomed to that tradition."

She stepped lightly as they continued, a weightlessness in her limbs, a sense of breathlessness she couldn't describe. Or maybe she could. She was content. Truly content.

She tilted her head. "Although I've watched *The Big Sleep* at least a half dozen times, I never tire of watching it."

He nodded, seeming to know precisely what she meant.

Pausing at a street corner, he gestured upward and pointed out Orion, the hunter, the brightest constellation in the sky. He shared his enthusiasm for the stars with her, just as he had the night they went star gazing, bringing to mind an amazing memory and poignant tears. She loved everything about this man.

He tipped up her chin. "Why are you crying? Is anything wrong?"

"I'm not crying because I'm sad." She leaned into his chest. "I'm crying because I'm happy."

As they went on, he asked, "What was your favorite scene in the film?"

"There are several, but I always chuckle when Philip Marlowe first meets his daughter, Vivien. He mentions not being very tall and walking on stilts."

"And Vivien coolly informs him that stilts won't help." Lorenzo chuckled. "The dialogue in the entire film is flawless."

Julie nodded in agreement. Perhaps it was the late hour, or the exhaustion from an incredibly busy day, or the fact that she felt so close to him, but it struck her that she should be totally honest with him. Therefore, she decided to challenge him with a question she'd reflected on all evening.

"Don't you like my family?"

He stopped and regarded her with a slight frown. "Why on earth would you ask me that question?"

"Because you were ... standoffish with them."

"I'm a loner, Julie. I told you that."

"But if you don't want to be with my family, then that affects me."

"I never said I didn't want to hang out with your family."

You acted it, she thought, but didn't express her observation aloud. Most likely, she was reading into actions and words that weren't there. Again, she blamed her reservations on weariness. Why had she brought up the subject? The evening had been perfect until then.

"What did you think of my sister Sally?" she asked.

"She seems nice. We only chatted alone for a couple minutes."

"Yes." Julie raised an eyebrow.

He paused, apparently choosing his words carefully. "From our discussion, she's totally invested in her daughter, her family and the chocolate shop."

"She's an entrepreneur and a hard worker."

"Another word to describe a workaholic."

She shot him an uneasy glance. "What's wrong with being a workaholic?"

"I'm tired of hearing about work, work, work. There's considerable more to life. When I'm in Italy, the pace is slower. Italians take their time eating, drinking and socializing."

"Well, some of us haven't had the opportunity to travel to Italy."

"And others," he firmly reminded, "were specifically invited. I believe I'm still waiting for a favorable response."

She rubbed her forehead, realizing she should answer him. "I'll know more after the first of the year." Her reply was noncommittal. She knew it, and so did he. "Let's see how it goes."

How what goes? Their relationship? How her restaurant fared? She didn't elaborate.

He offered a cool smile, his posture stiff and proud. "Right."

*B*y noon, Julie stopped into The Pasta Junction's kitchen, soon flanked by two of her finest cooks, one being Antonio, her sous chef. While they engaged in the preparation of meatballs, baked chicken, and fried sausage and peppers for Lorenzo's party, she readied her homemade fettuccini.

She insisted on preparing the cassata herself, cracking eggs, chopping maraschino cherries, stirring the ingredients together, and applying some of Lorenzo's suggestions for interpreting his grandmother's recipe by using exact measurements.

But then she resisted. He used math to figure precise quantities, but they'd tested his method and he still hadn't been satisfied. The man was never content when it came to this dessert.

Sally had insinuated that it was more—his excuse to see Julie.

Perhaps. She set down the mixing spoon and stared at the cake mix box.

But there was more.

When he'd described his grandmother's cassata, waxing poetic about her cozy kitchen, the rich scent of chocolate chips, he'd actually hummed and begun singing in Italian.

Realistically, however, he wouldn't remember how the dessert tasted. He was seeking to recapture an ideal moment from his childhood. That's what he was after.

The memories. The good times framed forever in his mind.

A half hour before Lorenzo's family was scheduled to arrive, nervous anticipation brought an emptiness to the pit of Julie's stomach.

Suppose his mother didn't approve of her? Or what if his family didn't like her restaurant, or the special buffet and dessert she'd prepared?

Quickly, she changed out of her work attire. Lorenzo had invited her to the party, insisting she attend as a guest, and not a hostess who would serve them. This caused even more of a panic. She'd literally be sitting down to a meal with them.

She closed her eyes and breathed a calming breath.

For the event, she'd chosen a knee-length dress in a shimmering silver and high heel pumps. She left her hair loose, the way Lorenzo preferred, and it fell over her shoulders in loose waves.

Of course, there was also a feeling of panic because of the man himself, she thought, as she clipped on a pair of sparkly earrings. They hadn't parted on good terms. He usually texted her in the morning, and his texts, which she'd read with a racing heart, had been short:

Happy New Year, Julie.

She responded with the same greeting.

Do you need any help today? I'm happy to come to the restaurant early. I'm done at the station by noon. I can assist you with the cassata preparation.

Thanks. I'm all set. She'd cringed after she'd sent the message. Did it sound like she didn't need his help ... that she didn't need *him*?

Okay, came his response.

She wondered if he was really okay with her answer.

My staff volunteered to come in early, she quickly texted, as a way to assuage her reply with an explanation. *Thanks anyway.*

See you at three o'clock, then.

She typed *Great,* changed it to *Good,* and hit send.

After she freshened her lipstick, she read through his texts again. Their exchange had been systematic. Dejectedly, she blew out a sigh, remembering the slightly sour ending to their evening. She didn't have enough experience with relationships, and as swift as their attraction had been, there was plenty yet to learn about each other.

With a final determined breath, she inspected herself in the full-length mirror in the restroom, and headed for the private dining area for the final arrangements.

When Lorenzo's family arrived a few minutes later, his mother, a tiny slim woman, swept into the room, surrounded by four men, one woman, and two giggling children.

The way Lorenzo's mother carried herself brought poise to her effortless beauty. As Lorenzo took the lead, presenting his mother as Mrs. Eleanor Talley to Julie, her motions were graceful.

She held Julie's hand firmly for several seconds before letting go. "I've heard a great deal about you." Her gray eyes, with flecks of gold and brown, emanated warm kindness. "My son spoke about you nonstop when he visited my husband and me in Wyoming."

"Did he?" Bewildered laughter stole into Julie's tone.

"Thanks for giving away all my secrets," Lorenzo said before focusing on Julie. "Happy New Year."

The husky resonance in his tone drew a sharp wrench to her heart.

"Happy New Year, Lorenzo."

"You are beautiful."

"Thank you. And you are dashing."

Already, he'd taken off his suit jacket and rolled his white shirtsleeves back.

"Lorenzo, we haven't taken any pictures yet," his mother chided.

"I'll put my jacket back on for pictures, Ma," he replied.

From beneath her long lashes, Julie studied him. He caught her gaze and smiled, and she was fully aware of the magnetism drawing them together.

He broke the spell by doubling back to an elderly balding man with a neat white mustache. "May I introduce my stepfather, Joe Talley? He's brought my mother tremendous happiness and we're pleased to all be present for their first wedding anniversary."

"Julie, your restaurant is magnificent," Eleanor remarked, as Lorenzo rushed away to dash after the twins, who were taking turns jumping off a side chair. "Believe me, my family knows a lot about running a restaurant."

"You do?" Julie asked.

"Yes, my late husband owned a restaurant for a short spell. Didn't Lorenzo mention it to you?"

Unpleasantly surprised, Julie shook her head. "No, he never breathed a word."

"It was only for a matter of months. Just long enough to ensure we all lost money before his next venture." With a dismissive wave, Eleanor redirected her attention to the group. "Thank you, Lorenzo, for all your planning, and to my lovely daughter and her husband and children, and my son, John."

Regina, Lorenzo's sister, gave a friendly wave, then attempted to catch up to her twin girls who were chasing each other around the room.

Lorenzo returned and guided his mother and stepfather

to the head of the table, which Julie had decorated in gold. The table featured a large pansy flower bouquet centerpiece, the vivid purple and bright yellow blossoms brilliantly displayed in an antique cream-colored teapot. From the ceiling, Julie's staff had hung gold balloons and streamers. The traditional colors and flowers celebrated a first anniversary.

John stepped up to Julie and took her cold hands in his. "Now that wasn't so bad, was it?" he teased.

"I'm thrilled to meet your family."

"Good, because we're happy to meet you too." Like his older brother, John was tall and slim, and his dark good looks heightened the similarity between them. However, John's eyes were a soft gray, the same color as his mother's, and his presence wasn't as powerful as Lorenzo's. He possessed a tranquil quality, but still exuded his brother's charm in equal measure.

"I hope to make a good impression," Julie admitted.

"For Lorenzo's sake."

"For all of you," she clarified.

At the sound of Eleanor's voice, everyone swung toward her in unison. "And now," she declared as the waitstaff set up the buffet's silver trays, "*mangiamo*. Let's eat."

Tempting aromas of basil, garlic, peppers, and tomato sauce filled the intimate room, and everyone heartily agreed.

*L*orenzo invited Julie to sit next to him at the round table they all shared. He was confused by the distance she maintained between them, which seemed odd considering her delighted expression when his mother had remarked that he'd spoken about Julie nonstop.

Throughout dinner, he methodically reexamined their whirlwind courtship, seeking a clue, a detail in one of their conversations. Perhaps he'd miscalculated the deepness of her feelings for him, although she'd responded to his kisses with sweet abandonment, and consistently seemed pleased to see him.

By the time the meal was finished, he'd only come up with pleasant images of their moments together. Julie was kind and good-hearted, radiating a generous spirit.

Was she afraid of a commitment? If so, he understood. Sally had revealed to him in their short two minutes together that Julie had been hurt by a married man.

"We're ready for dessert!" His sister's twin girls interrupted his musings, loudly chanting when the waitresses brought out two perfect cassatas arranged on white bento boxes. The staff placed both boxes by Lorenzo's mother.

He grinned, reveling in her exclamations of delight. When she tasted the cassata, she'd remember ...

Emma—her curly hair the only distinguishable characteristic between her and her straight-haired twin, Ella—raced from her seat. Before anyone could react, she reached up to the table and yanked one of the boxes. The cassata landed on the floor and split in two.

Julie quickly rose, and he drew her back down. "Allow your staff to handle it. We'll eat the other cassata."

As one waitress cleaned up the mess, the other sliced the cheesecake and delivered the first piece to his mother on a gleaming plate. Lorenzo watched her intently, waiting for her reaction.

"Delicious!" She smiled at Julie. "You baked this?"

Julie blushed gorgeously. "Yes. Do you like it?"

"I love it!"

His mother took another bite, but didn't dissolve into tears, as he'd half-expected. Maybe her mother's cassata hadn't been as important to her as it had been to him.

"Is anything the matter?" Julie asked him, as she accepted her plated cassata from a server.

"I'm surprised," he said.

"Are you surprised the cassata turned out so well?"

"You're a mastermind in the kitchen." He sampled a bite and closed his eyes, almost dropping his fork. Yes, whatever Julie had created, she'd managed to bring alive the memories of his youth.

"Is this the part where I'm supposed to offer a clever rejoinder?" she teased. "Perhaps another weatherman joke?"

He laughed. "I'll wait for your brother for that."

Much to his relief, her eyes twinkled. Slowly, he felt her tenseness begin to melt away.

He set his fork beside his plate as the lights dimmed, and a 1940s song began to play, *I'm in the Mood For Love*. His heart burst with pride. Julie had organized every detail to ensure the party's success.

Lorenzo's stepfather and mother found a modest space on the floor to dance. The twins gleefully joined in, holding hands and twirling round and round.

Julie chuckled. "They're adorable and exactly how you described."

He glimpsed her profile. Her head was turned away, her hands folded in her lap.

"And so are you." He placed an arm around her shoulders.

"I'm adorable?"

"Absolutely."

She granted him a sidelong glance and sidled closer. "And you're the most charming man I've ever met."

"Excellent, because I hope to occupy many hours of your time." Gently, he stroked her hair. "That is, if it's okay."

"It's okay."

"Look, I'm sorry about what I said ... about your family. They're a fun bunch."

She gazed up at him. "They mean the world to me. I love

every minute with them and want to share those moments with you."

Because she cared.

"Only on one condition," he warned.

"What's that?"

"You'll spend time with my family as well. Agreed?"

She brought a heartwarming smile to her nod. "Agreed."

"And there's another thing," he added.

"What's that?"

"How about a little trip to Italy with me?"

She gave him a questioning look. "You still want me to go?"

"Absolutely."

"Then I gladly accept. I'm looking forward to knowing you better in the new year. Everything about you."

"I feel the same way about you." He smoothed a kiss on her temple. "Any more good news?"

Her beautiful eyes widened. "I'm adopting a dog."

"A male?"

"Yes. His name will be Buddy."

This was his Julie. Taking time to mull things over, then coming to a decision when she was ready.

"I love you," he softly said.

Her reaction was thoughtful, bringing a firm tug to his heart. "I love you too."

"You know," he said, "I was thinking about that dame upstairs."

"Think no more. I'm right beside you."

And that's where he intended her to stay. Beside him, where she belonged.

Their new beginning, a fresh start, brought a mistiness to his eyes.

Because a beautiful, precious woman, the woman he loved, had strolled into his peaceful life.

And she had brought with her a bright future, full of limitless possibilities.

HE END

A NOTE FROM JOSIE

Dear Friends,

Thank you for reading *A Chocolate-Box New Years*.

I wanted to write a holiday romance centering around chocolate.

If you loved this sweet romance as much as I loved writing it, please help other people find *A Chocolate-Box New Years* by posting your review.

A Chocolate-Box New Years is available in ebook, paperback, audiobook, and Large Print paperback.

Want the individual books of the Chocolate-Box Series? Click here.

And be sure to read: A Chocolate-Box Summer Breeze

I'd love to meet you in person someday, but in the meantime, all I can offer is a sincere and grateful thank you. Without your support, my books would not be possible.

As I write my next sweet or inspirational romance, remember this: Have you ever tried something you were afraid to try because it mattered so much to you? I did, when I started writing. Take the chance, and just do something you love.

My Spotify Play List for A Chocolate-Box New Years is here.

With sincere appreciation,

Josie Riviera

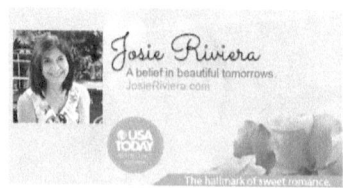

RECIPE FOR GRANDMA GLORIA'S CHEESECAKE CASSATA

Ingredients:

Marble Cake Mix

2 lbs. coarse ricotta cheese (use low or non-fat if you prefer)

½ cup sugar

4 eggs

1 cup chocolate chips, or more.

1 cup maraschino cherries-chopped, or less.

Instructions:

Follow recipe on cake mix box. Place in a greased cassata or sturdy angel food cake pan.

Blend the rest of the ingredients together and place on top of prepared cake mix.

Bake at 350 degrees for 1 ½ hours.

Let set for 2 hours. Better when refrigerated.

USA TODAY BESTSELLING AUTHOR

JOSIE RIVIERA

a Chocolate-Box Valentine

PRAISE AND AWARDS

USA TODAY bestselling author

Top 15 Amazon Bestseller Family Life Fiction

Top 20 Amazon Bestseller Saga Fiction

Top 20 Amazon Bestseller Romance Anthologies

CHAPTER ONE

*I*t was raining. Again. Hard and relentless.

Sally Elliot gazed out the window of Blooming-field Candy Shop, the shop that she'd owned for nearly a decade.

From high school onward, she'd become passionate about candy making and dedicated all her efforts into turning her dream into a reality. She'd prided herself on her strong work ethic, because surely success would follow. And her shop wasn't a franchise. The shop was her *own* business, started from scratch.

However, as in the case of many newbie business owners, she'd overestimated her sales and underestimated her costs.

Yet, her perseverance had eventually paid off.

Or rather, her perseverance *usually* paid off, except that ... Well, except that if today was any indication of candy sales for the month of February, she was skating directly toward a patch of thin ice. If she plunged through, she'd be out of funds within six months.

With a nervous sigh, she glanced out the front window of her shop.

Anxious thoughts clustered in her mind, as they invariably did when sales were slow, and she did her best to banish them. It was a gray, rainy and steely afternoon. Therefore, she attributed the lack of sales to the bad weather.

Okay, fine. She turned away from the window. She could deal with bad weather.

However, she couldn't deal with the fact that the delivery of the specialty chocolate she'd ordered, in fact, *needed*, was late. Not thirty minutes late, or an hour, but an entire half day. And this was a rush supply, because she had underestimated the amount of candy that customers would pre-order for Valentine's Day.

She'd read in a business magazine that fifty-eight billion pounds of chocolate were purchased during Valentine's week. Well, she was nowhere near selling that amount.

Still, her store sold a lot of candy.

Ben, her older brother, stood beside a white display case in the middle of the store, holding his cellphone to his ear. He offered a trace of a smile, then sobered. His gaze flicked from her to the free foil-wrapped candy kisses they offered to customers near the cash register. Gift cards were also conveniently stacked for last-minute buyers, who were mostly men.

Sally shook her head. Surely there was some psychology behind that. Perhaps men didn't embrace the shopping experience like women did. Or perhaps they were procrastinators, because they didn't have the right mindset to shop.

She wouldn't know. She hadn't been part of the dating scene for many years. In fact, because she'd married so young, had she ever been part of the scene?

Ben muttered into his cellphone, glanced at her, and then away again. She blinked in confusion at his somber expression, pressing away the prickle of awareness that something might be wrong.

No. This day couldn't possibly get any worse.

She walked to the front of the store. The vibrant red lollipops, balloons and gaily packaged gifts she'd added to the entryway brought a grin to her face. Several displays enhanced the different types of chocolate in the shiny cases lining the walls, and all reflected the upcoming Valentine celebration. As a savvy businesswoman, she recognized that placing beautiful and enticingly wrapped candy boxes where they would easily be seen resulted in impulse buys.

She'd been pleased with the result, though now she wasn't so sure.

Was the staging too white? Too red? Too cutesy? Had the displays put buyers off from entering the store today?

Thoughtfully, she nibbled on her lower lip as she second-guessed herself.

Ben ended his conversation, then jammed his cellphone into his pocket.

She turned to him. "Are you finally finished with your conversation?"

"Yep." His voice was quiet, his gaze probing. "And can you do anything else besides look worried?

Her seasoned eyes took in his uneasy expression. "Can you do something besides acting so secretive?"

"Okay, that's a fair question," he said, "but I expect an answer from you first."

"Why?"

"Because I asked you first."

"Alright." She shifted. "Does my nervousness show because of our lack of customers today?"

"A little. Actually, more than a little." His unswerving stare unnerved her. "You don't seem to enjoy anything fun anymore. Often, Maise and I have invited you to dinner, and you consistently refuse."

"What does that have to do with my looking nervous?"

"Everything. Your business shouldn't be the focus of your entire life."

"It isn't," she answered with a self-conscious laugh. "My daughter is."

"Along with your business."

"This conversation isn't fair, Ben. The biggest candy holiday of the year is looming and I can't deal with any more guilt. I'm extremely busy right now."

"You're always busy because you're a workaholic."

"Please, Ben, not again, although I realize you mean well." Sally stood straight in open rebellion, using the cool business tone she usually reserved for her suppliers when she haggled over snagging the best prices. "You and Maise can invite me when Valentine's Day is over. I guarantee I'll say yes."

"We'll see."

Despite the five-year age difference between them, their features were similar—both blue eyed, tall and lean. However, that was where the similarities ended, because Sally had been a tangle-haired blond adventurer in her youth, whereas dark-haired Ben was a stickler for following rules.

Nonetheless, Ben was her financial as well as emotional support. When her daughter, Clarissa, had been born prematurely, so tiny and swaddled in pink chenille blankets in a hospital isolette, her husband, Leon, had deserted them. At the tender age of twenty, Sally had become a single mother and consequently depended on Ben and her two sisters, because Leon had disappeared from her life. Several years later, nothing had changed except for her hasty divorce.

Once, as a teenage girl harboring romantic fantasies, she'd assumed that she and Leon shared a love that endured forever. After all, they'd dated since high school.

She'd been wrong.

For better or for worse. She shook her head in mock disgust at her naïve illusions.

"So on February fifteenth," Ben said, "you'll revert back to the optimistic sister I formally knew?"

"You've known me all your life."

"I mean the fun-loving adventurous girl before you became an entrepreneur." At her frown, he hastily explained, "Which will be great, because I've never seen you this jumpy and anxious, not even during the Christmas holiday candy season."

Sally stooped to rearrange the trail of pink and lavender paper hearts she'd secured to the front window. With dismay, she realized that one of the hearts had torn. Did she have any extra hearts left? She scrambled to her feet, intending to rummage through the back storage room.

"I'm jumpy and anxious," she clarified, "because I need that case of specialty chocolate for my newest candy-making project. And you still haven't answered *my* question, Ben. You're looking so ... secretive." Ben's gaze was downcast as she rushed past him. He didn't reply, but her mind was already racing toward the next task. "Moonglow Chocolatiers supplies the finest chocolate and I'm depending on them to come through with my rush order."

"You don't *need* specialty chocolate," Ben said. "You *want* specialty chocolate."

She swung around. "I've advertised my new chocolate creations since January, and there are outstanding orders. Not to mention our walk-in customers between now and February fourteenth. I can't produce dark shells for salted caramel infusion candy without bittersweet chocolate."

"What is infusion candy, anyway?"

"I explained to you yesterday. It's—"

"I remember."

"Do you, truly?"

"Well, I remember the candy part." He threw up his hands. "I admit my knowledge of candy would fit into—"

"A peanut butter cup."

"Right." He smirked. "But as co-owner of your shop, I have permission to be concerned about you. You're spending excessive time and energy focusing on your latest product and you're exhausted and overwhelmed."

"Once I hire the two additional new employees—"

"Both of whom you haven't found yet."

She pushed out a breath. "Then I'll be able to relax."

He quirked a dark eyebrow. "You're a go-getter, but lately you've taken on too much of the workload yourself."

"We own a candy shop, Ben. Valentine's Day is a significant holiday in our world."

"Why not promote our signature chocolate coffee fudge, instead?" He scanned the row of sugar-coated candy apples and the popcorn machine she'd recently placed next to the fudge presentation. "Our fudge won first place at the women's shelter candy-making contest in December, and since then sales have doubled."

Sally eyed the red and white bento boxes chock-full of their number one selling fudge positioned at the entrance. "Thanks to your fiancée, Maise."

"I attribute our success to your candy-making skills. Maise simply wrote an outstanding newspaper article that helped bring in customers."

"She also awarded our fudge first place."

"Maise wasn't the only judge at the women's shelter contest. The other two judges voted for our chocolate too."

Ben's cellphone rang, and he fished in his pocket.

"Again?" Sally asked.

With a quick nod, Ben flipped open the phone and swiveled from her.

When he finished speaking, he fidgeted, placed his phone on the counter next to the cash register, then unwrapped a candy kiss.

Sally's gaze shifted from the candy kiss to Ben. "Who called this time?"

"The same person as last time."

"And that same person is—?"

He popped the candy kiss into his mouth. "Do you want to sit down first?"

Her response was an exasperated glance. "I'd rather stand."

"Your specialty chocolate shipment is delayed. That was Joe, the delivery man. He phoned earlier too."

"Joe? Why? What happened?"

"We were trying to work out a plan, unfortunately without success." Ben chewed the candy, swallowed, then displayed a bright smile. "No use in fretting, though. Our store has plenty of chocolate to carry us through Valentine's Day."

Fretting? *Fretting?* Ben never used words like that. This was his way of avoiding, then softening the news she didn't want to hear. She stepped to the counter and concealed her distress by taking a brisk swallow of coffee that had turned cold. She grimaced. "Exactly how late is the shipment?"

"Joe's truck broke down in Evanville and he's grounded at a diner called Olive's. More significant is an update that the major highways are flooding."

She frowned and drew her cellphone from the pocket of her black slacks, scrutinizing the weather map. "Heavy rain is in the forecast, but the storm is west of here."

Her brother's penetrating blue eyes leveled on her. "Which means?"

"I'll get the order myself. That way, I can return to the shop tonight and begin making infusion candy." As he shook his head she reminded, "Outstanding orders to fill, remember?"

He didn't bother to assure her that she was right. He merely blew out a sigh.

"Will you pick up Clarissa?" Sally grabbed her pink water-repellent jacket from the coat rack and slid on a pair of yellow rain boots. "School dismisses at three o'clock."

"Certainly." Ben nodded. "Provided you give Maise and me permission to take her to dinner. We may head to The Pasta Junction and see Julie. Lorenzo will be there after he gets off work at the television station."

Julie, their sister, owned The Pasta Junction. Lorenzo Rossi was the local weatherman, and they'd been dating for a few weeks. They'd met when he booked her restaurant for a first wedding anniversary dinner, a surprise for his mother and new husband. Over the excuse of baking the perfect Italian cassata cheesecake, Lorenzo had seen Julie several times, and they'd dated ever since.

They both shared a variety of commonalties—their appreciation for fine food, all things Italian, and film noir, which Sally had never watched, although Julie and Lorenzo raved about the stylistic black-and-white films.

Someday, perhaps, when she had more time, Sally promised herself.

Pulling her attention to the present, she said, "Dinner for my daughter is mac and cheese. Nothing fancy. Believe it or not, Clarissa also likes steamed broccoli."

"Can you repeat where you're headed?" Ben asked.

"Olive's Diner." Sally caught her brother's concerned stare. "I'll return by eight o'clock tonight."

"Stick to the main route, 29A. And check Lorenzo's weather forecasts."

"I will. And stop worrying, big brother. I'll call Joe and meet him at the diner." Sally schooled her features into a reassuring smile, waved her cellphone in the air, and scurried out the door.

CHAPTER TWO

*I*f there was one thing Sally loved about Valentine's Day, it was chocolate. She sold the idea, the rich, velvety taste, to her customers—celebrating romance by gifting exquisite candy to a spouse or partner, or any loved one.

The entire holiday was appealing, although a man's love was something she hadn't experienced in ages. If ever, if she was honest with herself. The holiday had lost all significance when her ex-husband had bailed on her and their daughter. He'd gotten a preview of the responsibility of caring for a premature infant, which meant little sleep and a selfless attitude, and he'd wanted no part of it.

So much for a dedicated partner and lifelong commitment.

She sighed as she surveyed the wet roads ahead.

Lorenzo had predicted rough weather, the message flashing across her cellphone screen. Sometimes he was right, other times wrong. This time, unfortunately, he was right.

The lengthy day was taking its toll, and six o'clock showed on her car's dashboard by the time she neared the diner. Joe, the delivery driver, had acknowledged her phone call with gratefulness, and assured he'd meet her in the parking lot.

Dusk fell early on a chilly, rainy day in California, and the evening had darkened sooner than Sally anticipated. A slow-moving thunderstorm had followed her, and there had been no break in the icy-gray clouds. Mercilessly, rain pounded her windshield, and the concrete highway became slick, then muddied. As she drove, her gaze flicked repeatedly to the edge of the road as she dodged sizable tree branches.

She gripped the steering wheel tight against the blustery wind swaying her car, tuned her car radio to a traffic station and was immediately bombarded by a series of flash-flood warnings.

"Travelers on route 29A are advised to choose another route." The announcer issued the advisory in a somber tone.

Her car crested the last hill. A neon sign back-lit in green blinked *Olive's Diner*, and soft light beckoned from the large paneled windows. The exterior walls in reflective silver reminded her of a favorite 1950s diner she'd frequented as a child, and she anticipated a blue plate special of savory meat loaf and creamy mashed potatoes, topped with homemade brown gravy.

She drove into the parking lot, relieved to spot the Moon-glow Chocolatiers truck. The driver's door snapped open and a short, stocky man slid out. Wearing eyeglasses and a jovial expression, he hailed her. "Sally Elliot?"

She zippered up her raincoat, secured the hood, and stepped from her car. Several other vehicles, including an outdated pickup truck, were parked nearby.

"I'm here!" she called as he darted toward her. Horizontal, icy pellets of rain whirled around them.

"I'm Joe." He gestured upward. "The tree branches are swinging like crazy. I heard on the radio that the wind gusts could reach forty miles per hour."

She brushed away the cold raindrops hitting her cheeks, tightened the raincoat's hood sheltering her head, then jammed her hands into her pockets. "Yes, I heard the same."

"I'll hurry and load the chocolate into your car, ma'am. Thanks for driving here."

"You're welcome." *Really, she'd had no choice, because she needed the chocolate now.* "I didn't want this shipment delayed another day." She peered toward the road. Here in the blinding rainstorm, everything blurred.

"As soon as you're finished, I'll be on my way back to Bloomingfield," she said. "If it's okay, I'll stay in my car to avoid the rain."

A cracking sound, then a creak, prompted them both to spin. A gigantic tree fell across the highway with a crash resembling a thunderous roar. It was so close that, for several seconds, Sally feared the diner had been hit.

Fortunately it hadn't.

However, the tree blocked her way home.

In the ensuing seconds of stunned silence, she heard herself gasp, scarcely audible above the whistling wind. A chill shivered up her spine as noise and chaos erupted around her.

A young couple rushed out of the diner. They gaped in disbelief at the fallen tree, shouting in shrill voices that they were phoning the police while signaling to Sally and Joe to hurry inside.

Joe's eyes widened as he gaped at the wide tree limbs spread across the road. "Wow, that's a huge tree. You won't be returning to Bloomingfield tonight," he said. "Let's get inside with the other stranded folks."

For a few seconds, Sally lacked the ability to utter a coherent sentence. Absently, she rubbed her arms, then reached inside her car to retrieve her tote bag.

The only word she'd heard was *stranded*. With an unfocused stare, she darted a gaze toward the tree, then Joe, then the diner. The neon green sign was still blinking, so the diner hadn't lost power.

"You'll like the cook," Joe was saying. "We chatted before you arrived, and he's a good guy."

No, no, no. Good guy or not, this tree had to fall now? The same question raced over and over in her mind.

"The cook. Right," she tonelessly replied, realizing her voice shook. "Where is he? Didn't he hear the noise?" She dragged her thoughts from a situation she couldn't control and sprinted with Joe across the parking lot.

"Okay, Olive," she muttered to herself as they entered and stamped their wet boots in the entryway. "I hope you serve meat loaf." She envisioned a burly cook sporting a straggly white beard, a dirty apron tied around his protruding belly.

Joe shrugged off his jacket and swung it over a coat rack. He beamed at a well-dressed woman and slid into her booth. Eagerly, his voice raised above Elvis Presley crooning from the wall-mounted juke box, as Joe embellished the events that had taken place. The young couple that had raced outside were already snuggled in a corner booth. They bid Sally a quick wave.

"Are you all right?" the young woman asked. Her mid-length chestnut-colored hair was damp from the rain. On her porcelain cheeks was a hint of red blusher.

"Yes, yes, I'm fine." Sally offered a nervous laugh, then raised her voice for the benefit of the man who had emerged from the kitchen and had begun brewing coffee behind the counter. "Oh, hello."

He curved around. "Hi. Glad you were able to get out of the rain."

Rain? His calm statement snapped the last thread of her reserve. "Are you aware a tree fell in front of the diner?"

"Yes. I was in the back room when it happened. The police have been called. You're safe here."

"Safe?" she parroted, surveying the oversized booths with seats covered in green plastic. The pink lights shining over each booth cast the diners in rose-colored puddles of light. "This diner could blow ... all the way to Kansas."

"No wicked witches here, and I assure you that you're not in Oz," the man countered. "This building has been standing here for a hundred years, and will be here long after we're gone."

"Now that's reassuring."

"No worries." His tone was composed, his manner amiable.

The first thing she noticed about him was his eyes. They were a wonderful hazelnut brown, shining and welcoming. He wore a smile which he freely extended. He was tall, muscular, and well-toned.

"I assume you're the cook?" she asked.

"Yes."

"Is the owner here?"

He sent her a brief grin. "You're looking at him."

Her lips parted. He looked too young to own a restaurant. She guessed him to be in his midthirties. But then again, she was young too, approaching thirty, having opened her shop several years earlier.

She tugged off her raincoat and draped it over a stool, apologizing for the puddle pooling on the black-and-white square tile flooring beneath her feet.

"It's all right. Tile is easy to clean." He gestured outside to the incessant rain. "I'm surprised anyone is out driving on a night like this."

"Well, I had no choice." She again glanced about the diner, at the youthful couple nestled close together in their booth and the smartly dressed older woman wearing camel wool slacks and a cream-colored cardigan. She'd been sitting alone before Joe took a seat across from her. Now they were thoroughly engaged in conversation and didn't seem to notice anyone else.

"I don't know about the others," Sally continued. "I'm sure they have their reasons for being here."

"It's probably because of my food." The owner's lips quirked into a smile. "Why else would anyone venture out in a severe storm?"

"Chocolate," Sally murmured. "If they desperately needed a shipment of chocolate."

"Ah, chocolate, the ideal sweet treat." Amusement laced his deep voice. She noted that he didn't remark on her use of the word *desperately*. "But you can't beat a diner for a plentiful, wholesome American meal."

"Oh, but you can," she said.

"Excuse me?"

"I beg to differ. My sister, Julie, owns a fine dining establishment called The Pasta Junction. She serves homemade fettuccini."

"The restaurant is located in Bloomingfield, correct?"

"Yes, have you ever visited?"

"This diner keeps me in Evanville most days."

"My sister's latest addition is a brick pizza oven."

The result had been pizzas with a smoky wood flavor and charred crust that had quickly become a town favorite. Certainly, authentic Italian food beat a greasy diner any day.

When her gaze flew to his, she could tell by his smile that, to her intense relief, he hadn't read her thoughts.

"Emily comes here every evening and eats dinner." He gestured toward the booth where Joe and Emily sat.

"Rain or shine, apparently," Sally said.

"Apparently." He chuckled. "The kissing couple are on their honeymoon and were passing through town when the storm hit. They said they wanted to drive across America and discover new places—wherever their travels took them."

"They obviously aren't planners," Sally said.

"They told me they love being spontaneous."

"I prefer an organized agenda. I'm more productive and efficient that way." Sally turned toward the couple, then back to him. He was studying her with a concerned frown.

"Spontaneous individuals have more fun," he said.

"But planning ahead yields better results."

"Like encountering fallen trees, for instance?" he asked. "The best laid plans of mice and men often ..."

"Often go astray," she finished.

"Awry."

"Yes, well, I'm familiar with that saying." To avoid the debate, she shifted. "Do you have many steady customers?"

"Thankfully, yes."

"So it gets busy here at times?"

"At times." That smile again. For a long moment he studied her, a warm look in his eyes.

Without warning, her heart began beating uncontrollably.

"A calm and deliberate pace wins the race," he continued.

"Another saying?"

"One of my own. And, a well-fed, contented customer will return."

"That's two sayings."

He shrugged. "I suppose, but they're both important."

She started to contradict him. A quick pace wins the race, she wanted to inform him. Instead, she toyed with the leather tote bag slung over her shoulder.

"Do you agree?" he inquired.

"No, sorry, I don't. At least, not with your first saying. Calm and deliberate won't fly in our fast-paced world where customers are constantly in a hurry."

"We'll just have to agree to disagree, then."

This time she didn't respond immediately, her attention captivated by his tousled rich-brown hair and the shadow of a dark beard. High cheekbones and an angular jaw brought one thought to mind: he was beyond handsome, and because of her preoccupation with the fallen tree and her plans going off-center, she hadn't noticed his athletic good looks until now.

She flushed as they locked gazes. "If the saying applies to your diner, that's all that matters."

For you. Not for me.

She squinted at her watch, then at the bakery case filled with a selection of breads, including sourdough and whole wheat; a coconut layered cake and cherry pie; and a dozen chocolate chip cookies. She surveyed the fake potted lilacs adorning each booth, the thick tan-colored curtains hanging from the windows. An antique cash register was situated at the far end of the counter. Coins from the young couple jingled into the juke box as they picked out songs, and Dolly Parton replaced Elvis, singing about working nine to five.

"This is a nice highway for a diner," Sally remarked. Again, she shifted. Brilliant, Sally, just brilliant. Who used the word *nice* to describe a highway? She put on a smile. "Did you decorate the place yourself?"

"Hardly. My sister helped me." With an easy grace, he collected her coat and hung it on the rack by the door. "Please forgive my manners. I should have taken your coat sooner."

That wasn't his job, which she voiced aloud.

"My pleasure," he responded.

She trailed him and stole a glance in the mirror near the doorway, critically appraising her hair, which always curled when wet. She was forced to wait and see how it behaved when it dried and hoped that tonight it wouldn't spin into a super frizzy mess. Scrutinizing her reflection, she knew that the endless nights she'd worked late had deprived her of much-needed sleep, subsequently leaving shadows beneath her eyes.

The man turned, his smile ever-present.

She felt her cheeks heat.

"Is your name ... Olive?" she asked. *Another stroke of brilliant conversation, Sally. Surely he'd named the diner after his sister.*

"Nope. I'm Oliver Menroe."

"And your sister?"

"Her name is Amy." Those brown eyes of his, so cordial and reassuring. She couldn't drag her gaze away. "And you are ...?"

"Sally. Sally Elliot."

"*Miss* Sally Elliott?"

"Yes."

"I'm glad to hear that."

She paused, surprised by his remark, but decided it was nothing more than courteous flirtation with a potential customer. Still, her mind scrambled for a subject change. "So the name Olive is ...?"

"The name from the previous owners. They were Italian and thought *Olive* had a nice ring to it."

"Didn't you want to add the *r* to the end of the word when you bought the place? There's a big difference between Olive and Oliver."

"The customers don't mind. It's a standing joke around here." Oliver wiped his hands on his clean white apron. *Clean,* completely shattering her preconceived notions of a short-order cook working at a diner in the middle of nowhere.

She pulled her cellphone from her bag and dashed off a text to Ben, explaining she was detained because of a fallen tree, had met Joe, the delivery man, and that they were both safely inside Olive's Diner.

Give Clarissa my love, she finished. *Is she having fun?*

A blast, Ben replied. *She's devouring a box of specialty infusion chocolates. (Kidding, kidding.) Let me know when you get back on the road. Maise and I will take care of Clarissa tonight and put her to bed. I have a key to your apartment, so don't fret.*

Fret again. Sally grinned and thanked him.

She snapped the phone shut and excused herself to freshen up in the restroom, then reentered the dining room. Although the diner was somewhat rundown and the fan above her didn't appear to spin, none of this took away from the inviting interior. Enticing whiffs of freshly ground coffee and buttery yeast rolls made her mouth water. She hadn't eaten since noon, an eggplant parmigiana takeout sandwich from her sister Julie's restaurant, and a cup of cold coffee.

Oliver strode into the open adjoining kitchen and stirred an enormous pot on the stove. Then he returned to stand behind the counter.

Sally indicated the display case, because she loved sweets. "Do you bake, Oliver?"

"I outsource to a woman in town because I realized my limitations early on. Would you like a chocolate chip cookie?"

"Certainly." She settled on a stool. "Thank you."

"I have a Greek salad in the cooler that's all made up."

"Perfect." Gratefully, she accepted the cookie while he arranged and garnished the salad, then set it, a glass of water, and a white paper napkin from the dispenser in front of her.

She flattened the napkin on her lap and bowed her head to offer a prayer of thanks to God. "How long have you been in business?" she asked.

"Five years." He shifted and switched on the grill. "Do you like your eggs over easy? I use fresh ingredients from the locals. Farm-to-home is a term I employed before it became trendy."

"Scrambled eggs are my favorite, but I'm already enjoying a salad and cookie, remember?

"Indulge me."

Sally wasn't up to disputing with him. Besides, she was still hungry, and it was hard to resist the intoxicating aromas of fresh coffee, grilled hamburgers, and butter-topped biscuits. She took a swallow of water. "I like my eggs with toast. I love toast."

"Wheat or white bread?"

"Do you have rye bread?"

"Of course." An enigmatic lazy smile crossed his lips while he scanned her features. She had the surprising notion that he was delighted she was sitting and talking with him, a notion that was highlighted when he lifted a loaf of rye bread in the form of a salute. "May I say, Sally, that you look lovely when your blond curls frame your face."

Her pulse fluttered. She'd never been complimented by a man waving a loaf of rye bread, but somehow his comment meant a great deal.

Somehow, she knew his compliment was heartfelt.

Wait. She set down her glass. Her curls framed her face? That meant her hair was a mass of oversized, wiry waves. She yanked at a curl near her cheek and watched it spring back into place. She really needed to look into purchasing a hair straightener.

"Well, okay, thank you," she said softly, then dug into her salad.

"Can you give me a minute before I cook your eggs?" he asked.

"Absolutely. I need more than a minute to digest."

Oliver started toward the dining room with a pot of coffee, refilling cups and talking with the customers. There were only a handful, Joe and Emily and the newlyweds, but he treated each person as if they were the most important one in the room, stopping to listen, nodding and optimistically commenting.

"You don't employ anyone else, Oliver?" Sally asked when he came back behind the counter. As he poured coffee for himself, then set the pot on the burner, she noticed the way his white T-shirt fit across his broad shoulders. He was strong and muscular, as if he routinely exercised each day.

"I have a dishwasher, hostess, and several local waitresses," he replied. "Because those raindrops were getting as big as hailstones, I sent everyone home early."

Five minutes later, he set a plateful of steaming scrambled eggs, two slices of buttered rye toast, and a mug of coffee next to her salad. She eyed the mug, and he smiled. "I assumed you may want coffee, because it might be a long night."

"Thanks."

"Cream and sugar?"

"Black is fine."

"Me too." He rolled his coffee mug between his palms. "Joe and I chatted a while before you arrived. He told me you own a candy store, and he was on his way to deliver wholesale chocolate to you."

"Then you know my story."

"Yes, I expect I do, but I'm always interested in learning more."

About her?

She fell silent, sipping her coffee, and evaded questioning why he might be so interested. Perhaps he simply craved conversation. Long hours in a diner might cause him to become lonely and disconnected. Sometimes in her candy shop, a sense of isolation would sweep over her, prompting her to phone one of her siblings. She wondered if Oliver felt the same.

"There isn't much else to say," she replied.

He splashed more coffee into her mug. "I didn't mean about your business. I meant about you."

She gave a little laugh and decided to talk about her business again. "When Joe's truck broke down, he phoned my brother Ben. I drove here to pick up the chocolate for my special infusion candy, because I couldn't wait another day for the delivery."

Oliver popped two more slices of toast into the toaster, then regarded her. "Ironic, because the tree fell unexpectedly and you're delayed, anyway."

There was something about the matter-of-fact way he described her situation, something about his easy manner and intoxicating grin that triggered a sudden, irrepressible, and, considering the turn of events, curious response from Sally. She began chuckling. And then she began laughing so hard, tears coursed down her cheeks. Her ribs still hurt from laughing when Oliver walked over carrying another plate of buttered rye toast.

A minute later, he seated himself on a stool next to her with a second mug of coffee, joking with her because she couldn't choose between a slice of coconut layered cake or cherry pie for dessert.

"Try both." He swallowed some coffee and put the mug aside.

Deliberately, she turned to gaze at him. "Honestly, Oliver, you believe in feeding your customers extraordinarily well."

His gaze never left hers. "That's my saying, remember?" She smiled at his contagious good nature and attempted to match his humor. "One of your many sayings," she reminded.

He stood to clear away her dishes. "By the way, being that you seem to want to focus only on business, what is infusion candy?"

She laughed and dismissed his inquiry with a wave. "Never mind. Let's just say it's a fancy specialty candy."

With the plates in his hands, he paused to consider her—

from the top of her wavy hair which surely resembled a lion's mane by now, to the toes of her rain boots.

Another bewildering tingle went through her. She shook her head, mystified at her reaction to this man.

"You own Bloomingfield's Candy Shop," he said.

"Yes. I assumed you knew that from your conversation with Joe."

"I didn't piece everything together until now. Your picture and an article were featured in the newspaper at Christmastime. I thought I recognized you from somewhere." Across the two feet between them, their gazes held, the silence punctuated by the newlyweds giggling and smooching, Joe and Emily chatting quietly, and Patsy Cline singing from the juke box about falling to pieces. "In any event, we're both in the food service industry, so we can commiserate about the long hours. And speaking of which, I'd better put more coffee on."

Sally smiled as he stepped behind the counter, and she stood to wander to the window. Through the rain-streaked glass, she located the large tree, the lifeless limbs lying across the road. Fortunately, the Department of Transportation, truck lights flashing a dull yellow, had arrived.

After a few moments, Oliver walked over to join her.

"How long does it take to remove a tree?" she asked.

"First, the DOT will check to be sure the tree hasn't hit any power lines," he said. "We have power, so the electric company won't be called in."

"How long?" she repeated.

"Are you in a hurry?"

"You know I have a candy shop to run. More important, my seven-year-old daughter is at home. My brother and his fiancée are watching her tonight."

"You didn't mention you had a daughter. What's her name?"

"Clarissa." Sally pulled her cellphone from her pocket and scrolled through the pictures, opening a recent one where Clarissa, pink-cheeked and giggling, was sliding down a slide in the town park. Her hands were raised in utter delight. She'd skinned her knee that day, and Sally had held and comforted her in a steady grip, never wanting to let go.

"She's adorable." Oliver peered over her shoulder as she pointed to the photo. "As an aside, I thought you were a *miss*."

"I am." Sally slipped the cellphone back into her pocket. "I'm divorced."

"Me too. No kids for me, unfortunately."

Unfortunately? This tall, handsome man liked children? She couldn't stop from voicing her inquiry aloud.

"Of course. Who doesn't like children?" His expression gentled. "I wanted kids desperately. My ex-wife, however, had other plans, which included running off with my best friend."

"I'm sorry. Were you married long?"

"Two years. You?"

"I married my high school sweetheart." She sighed. "We were young, and when Clarissa came along ... It's complicated."

"That's life. In the end, it's all about living life and appreciating every moment."

This was the time for her to utter something profound and witty, but all she did was nod in agreement.

"Even if life is chaotic and unpredictable?" she asked.

"It's the journey that matters," he said softly.

She stared out the window at the rain streaming down the glass, the blinking yellow truck lights as crewmen moved debris to the grassy shoulder.

"At any rate," Oliver continued, "the DOT will cut the tree into pieces and stack it on the side of the road, which will be challenging, because this road isn't very wide. To answer your question, plan on a two-or three-hour wait, depending on how quickly the work progresses. The police must have directed traffic off the last exit."

Frustrated, she expelled an impatient breath.

"Can I get you more coffee?" He headed toward the counter.

"Thank you." She trailed him and reclaimed a stool.

He replenished her mug, then again carried the coffee pot from customer to customer, refilling their mugs, chatting, offering food. His manner was jovial and inviting. He focused his attention outward, on his customers, ensuring they were satisfied.

"Still hungry?" he asked, when he returned to Sally. "Can I get you anything else? I'm used to preparing a lot of orders quickly, but apparently not tonight."

"Honestly, I'm stuffed." She raised her mug in a toast. "My sincere compliments. Oliver. Everything you served is delicious."

"My world-famous vegetable soup will be done in a few hours. You can have a bowl then."

"World-famous?" she teased.

"Well, in this town, anyway."

"I'd love some, but I expect I'll be long gone by the time it's finished." She peered at her watch. "I meant to ask you earlier—no meat loaf and mashed potatoes on your menu?"

"Of course." He grinned. "It's not on the menu because customers know I have it."

"Telepathy?"

"Something like that." He laughed out loud, full and hearty. "I can heat a plateful, if you'd like."

She chuckled and patted her stomach. "Perhaps another day."

"I'll prepare any meal, if I have the ingredients on hand. That's my saying."

"I thought your saying was 'Calm and deliberate wins the race'?"

He shrugged.

Comically, she raised her eyebrows. "How about your other saying that a well-fed, contented customer will return?"

He seemed to be trying to keep his features straight. "I suppose I have three sayings, then."

She chuckled. "What's in your soup?"

"You name the vegetable—"

"Onions, celery ..." she began.

"And my homemade beef broth, potatoes and carrots." Lightly, he touched her arm before pointing to the kitchen. It was friendly and casual, yet her pulse fired into a tailspin. "Can you guess the best thing about my soup?"

"Oliver, I'm not good at guessing."

"Tonight, the soup is on the house." His grin was boyish for such a confident, compelling man. "In fact, everything I've provided is on the house."

"Absolutely not. I can pay for my own food."

"I insist."

"Why?"

"Because you're the prettiest woman I've seen all day." He dragged up a stool to perch closer to her. "Correction. You're the most beautiful woman I've ever met."

"And you're staring at me because—"

"I told you why."

Self-consciously, she patted her hair. Sure enough, it had frizzed. "Thank you," she murmured, although she suspected she'd never looked worse.

"Tell me again why you're so eager to get back to Bloomingfield?" he asked.

"My daughter Clarissa is reason number one."

However, contemplating the hundreds of jobs awaiting her made Sally anxious. She chewed her bottom lip and took in the diner's coziness, the patrons sipping coffee and speaking quietly among themselves. The unhurried pace was quiet and relaxing.

"From what I understand," Oliver said, "your daughter is safe with your brother and his date. So again, what's your hurry to travel on these unsafe roads?"

"My candy shop's orders have exploded since the December newspaper article, and I've publicized a unique new product, which is why I came here tonight. Joe's truck—"

Oliver's quick nod interrupted her. "I was delighted to hear his story."

He was a good listener. Not many men possessed that quality. Not many *folks* possessed that quality. Most wanted to talk only about themselves. But with Oliver, she felt like she could chat with him for hours.

"In summary, I have hundreds of orders." She stared at him, stared down at her coffee. She hadn't intended to talk about her shop, but the shop was always on her mind.

"Therefore, it's a bad thing to have all this new business and the subsequent profits that go along with it?"

"No, of course not." She grabbed a napkin from the dispenser and dabbed at her mouth. "You're an entrepreneur. You of all people should understand."

"Aren't you thrilled to earn a living doing what you love?"

"I'm extremely grateful. It's just that so many rely on me —my employees, my customers, and everyone else along the supply chain. It's an enormous responsibility."

He scrubbed a hand over his face. "Your candy shop sounds tremendously successful."

She paused, realizing her unintended implication—that because his diner was modest, he didn't have the same pressures she did.

"Oliver, I apologize," she said.

He eased the awkward moment with a smile, then answered the cellphone buzzing in his jean pocket. After an abrupt conversation, he clicked off the phone.

"Excuse me. I need to pull together an order for takeout."

"Go ahead. I'll attend to the customers."

"Thanks, Sally." Oliver excused himself and hastened into the kitchen.

CHAPTER THREE

*E*mily, who had been sitting with Joe, stood. She flattened the creases in her tailored slacks, and her booted heels assertively clicked on the tile floor as she made her way to Sally. Joe grabbed a newspaper and sank back into the booth.

"I'm Emily Varon, as you probably know." She accompanied her introduction with a vibrant smile and direct eye contact. Something about her understated beauty, the cream-colored wool cardigan contrasting with her dark skin, her friendly mannerisms and overall interest, made Sally feel at home.

"I'm Sally Elliot."

"It's lovely to formally meet you, Sally."

In view of Emily's gracious greeting, Sally extended a smile in return. "I admired your outfit when I walked in," she said. "You are stunning and entirely put together."

With a toss of perfectly coiffed platinum-silver hair, Emily chuckled and sat straight and proper on the stool next to Sally, her hands clasped neatly on her lap. "You mean for a woman of a certain age."

"What I meant was ... you carry an aura of self-confidence."

"At seventy years old, I'm finally content with myself. Along the way, I've learned that women are beautiful no matter their age." Emily motioned toward the honeymooners cuddling and kissing, whispering and laughing. Once in a while, they paused to take a selfie. "Earlier, those two told me they've been together from the time they were in high school. They'll share many joys and sorrows." Wistfully, she exhaled. "There's something magical about a first love."

Sally flinched. For her, the couple was a painful reminder of her own marriage gone wrong, and the emptiness that had followed her for years. Not once since the final evening when Leon left had she wept, but in turn, a massive weight of sadness and heartache had accumulated inside her.

"My experience with first love didn't work out," she said quietly.

"You were married?" Emily inquired.

"And divorced. I took my maiden surname. I'm an Elliot again."

"It's your last love who truly matters." Emily's blue-eyed gaze fixed on Sally, as if she were seeking something. "He's the man to treasure."

Sitting on the sidelines of love, Sally attempted a serene smile.

"I overheard some of your conversation with Oliver. I wanted to come over earlier, but you two were so intent on each other, I didn't want to interrupt."

Sally rolled her eyes, an attempt at dismissing any attraction she might feel for Oliver. "I wouldn't say that."

"I would." Emily flicked a glance toward the kitchen. "At my age, I don't apologize for eavesdropping. Perhaps you should get to know a person before deciding who they are."

"I agree." Sally pinched the bridge of her nose and briefly

closed her eyes. "My comments to him about my candy shop being so busy were thoughtless."

In all honesty, his remarks to her were insightful—about being grateful and connecting with men and women and families. He stirred her to reflect on where she put her energy these days. Orders were at an all-time high. So why was she stressed and unhappy?

An older couple wandered into the diner, and Sally stood, excusing herself from Emily and taking it upon herself to greet the couple. The man, she noted, walked with a shuffle and used a cane.

"Hello, and welcome to Olive's Diner. Please sit anywhere." Sally gestured to an empty booth near the juke box.

"We were stopped by the fallen tree." The woman shrugged off her tan-colored raincoat and draped it on the seat beside her. "We came off a side road, and the police refused to wave us any farther."

"Can I get you anything?" Sally asked. "Coffee? Food?"

"I'm starved." The man's spotted, aged hands splayed across his chest. "We drove quite a while."

"Harold, we were on the road ten minutes. We've been married over thirty years and rarely agree on anything." His wife snorted with dismissive amusement, then leaned back and pulled her thin mouth into a scowl. "I'll just have coffee."

There was no similarity between them, Sally thought, as sometimes happened when men and women were married a long time. The wife was thin, gray-haired, and under five feet tall, whereas her husband was a solid foot taller and at least one hundred pounds heavier.

"What do you have to eat?" the man asked.

"You've eaten too much today already," came his wife's reply.

He set his cane beside him and removed his cap, revealing

the polished brilliance of his bald head. "You call that bowl of cereal this morning a meal?"

"You're forgetting you ate a massive lunch."

"Let me see what the owner recommends." Sally held up the couple's bickering with a smile. "I'll return shortly."

When Sally stepped into the spotless kitchen, the mouth-watering aroma of vegetable soup flooded her nostrils. On a large stainless steel table, Oliver was arranging a dozen sandwiches, some with meat and cheese, others peanut butter and jelly, as well as apple slices and shortbread cookies. On the side were twelve bottles of water.

"That's quite a takeout order," she said.

"Cora, the friend who phoned, runs a daycare center not far from here," he replied. "She's in a frenzy because of the storm. I wanted to prepare food that appealed to everyone."

"Wow, I'm impressed at how quickly you worked."

"Thanks. That's why I'm called a short-order cook." A lazy smile swept over his face. "Everything under control out there?"

"Two more customers arrived. Can you suggest what I can serve? They can't decide."

"How about a couple of deli sandwiches and two slices of cherry pie?"

"I'll check." Sally scurried to the couple, got their drink orders and served them, then rushed back into the kitchen.

"They actually agreed," she joked. Quickly, she made up the two plates.

Meanwhile, Oliver, without rushing, deftly finished the sandwich preparation and began wrapping each in brown paper bags.

With a businesslike tenor in her voice, Sally asked, "Are you always this efficient?"

"Like everyone, I try my best."

This was Oliver, believing the good in everyone. She

studied him surreptitiously as she plated the couple's sandwiches, then sliced two pieces of cherry pie.

Their mood of quiet camaraderie as they worked together, along with his heart-stopping grin and relaxed bantering, left her oddly unwilling to leave the confines of the kitchen. She was drawn to him, more and more for every minute they spent together. She knew he was thoughtful and considerate, his actions compassionate and kind-hearted. Beyond his handsome physique was an innate quality—a genuine caring about people.

Reluctantly, she placed the sandwich plates and slices of pie on a tray and headed for the dining room.

"I'll be in as soon as these sandwiches are wrapped," Oliver said. "Thanks for taking care of the orders for me."

"Absolutely."

A car pulled into the parking lot, stopping in front of the door. A thirty-something woman rushed inside as Oliver appeared with an armload of brown bags.

"I'm almost done, Cora. Give me a couple more minutes." He gestured to Sally. "But first, let me introduce you."

"I know Cora and I'll take it from here." Emily slid from her stool and walked over to Cora and Sally as Oliver returned to the kitchen. "Cora runs the daycare in town, and all the children love her. My neighbor's kids are always thrilled when they're dropped off there."

Cora raked a hand through her glossy black hair, the short pixie cut accentuating her vivid amber eyes and creamy complexion. "I love watching these kids, they're like family to me. Some of them were a little frightened when the storm hit, but most are excited."

"Where are they now?" Sally asked.

"With my brother at the daycare. He helps me out sometimes."

"I have a daughter. Her name is Clarissa," Sally said. "She's not afraid of anything, except fireworks on the Fourth of July. Then she cries and puts her hands over her ears."

"What do you do to calm her down?"

"I give her a piece of fudge and tell her that it has a magical ingredient which will make her happy."

"Does it work?" Emily inquired.

"Most of the time. If anything, the candy distracts her," Sally said. "You see, I own a candy shop, thus a supply of chocolate fudge is usually in a box on my kitchen counter. Don't worry, Clarissa brushes her teeth afterward."

From the corner of her eye, Sally noted that a smiling Oliver had surfaced from the kitchen.

"Oliver, thank you," Cora said as he slipped the takeout containers into several bags. "The kids can't return home yet since their parents are trapped on the other side of that downed tree."

"Glad I can help. I'll carry these to the car for you."

"I'm fine, but thanks for your support." Cora drew a wallet from her purse. "How much do I owe you?"

"Nothing. My treat and my pleasure." As she left, his lips curved upward into a dazzling smile that he directed toward Sally. That smile—honest and sincere, with exactly the right touch of straightforwardness—prompted a warmth in the pit of her stomach. She was getting it: he had his community too. Moreover, his heart was generous and empathetic.

She returned his thoughtfulness with her own twinkling smile.

Emily swiveled to face Sally. "Explain what is so vitally important about this chocolate of yours that you had to come fetch it yourself."

"I'm creating an infusion candy which requires a certain type of bittersweet chocolate."

"What's infusion candy?" Emily crossed her arms. "Some sort of millennial fad?"

"No, it's not a fad. The process is somewhat complex, but the design is important. However, I'm not sure I'll get back to my store in time to produce all the candy."

"How about a trade?" Oliver still stood by the doorway with them. "You can use my kitchen to create your candy. Afterwards, you can try my soup, which I guarantee is the most delicious taste in the world."

"Better than my signature fudge?"

"Yup."

She shook her head. "I doubt you have everything I need for my specialty chocolates."

"How about regular candy?" He grinned. "Specialty is overrated."

"We like peanut butter cups," the honeymooners chimed from their booth. Apparently the patrons were delighted to listen to each other's conversations, Sally mused.

"I stock jars of peanut butter," Oliver said. "And I have a recipe from my sister that calls for margarine and graham crackers and semisweet chocolate chips."

"I'm a candymaker."

"Peanut butter cups are candy," Emily pointed out.

"But my infusion candy uses high-quality bittersweet chocolate."

"Yes, yes, so we've heard." Emily looked so determined that Sally peered at her with a mixture of laughter and surrender.

"I prefer store-bought chocolate chips, of which I have plenty," Oliver broke in. Gently, he touched Sally's cheek, guiding her to gaze at him. "Sally Elliot, I challenge you to prepare a batch of peanut butter cups in my kitchen. In fact, I predict our candy will be better than your infusion ... whatever."

"*Our* candy?"

"A blending of two magnificent cooks' expertise."

His blunt response made her laugh. Her spirit crazily soared. Despite the exhausting workdays, he'd thrown down a gauntlet she couldn't resist picking up.

Tamping down her smile, she quickly texted her brother, telling him she would be late. She looked up at Oliver. "In that case, I accept your challenge."

This was a decisive decision for her, and she could feel herself poised on the threshold of an unforgettable evening. Granted, she wouldn't be making specialty chocolate, but she was creating something better. Memories.

Since Leon, she'd held men at a distance, but with Oliver she felt safe. She enjoyed being near him—the way he put others before himself, his selfless manner, his witty responses. And the way he looked, as if he'd materialized from a Hollywood magazine with his effortlessly attractive features.

"Good. I'll help you." Oliver's mouth quirked in a smile. "We can enhance the semisweet with a few pieces of your fancy bittersweet candy if you'd like."

"And I'll pour our little group of diners more coffee while Joe gets your chocolate," Emily said.

Joe returned with a pound of chocolate and handed it to Sally, but Emily stopped him from continuing on into the kitchen by grabbing his hand and leading him to a booth. "You two go ahead," she directed Sally and Oliver. "We'll be your taste testers when you're done."

"Shall we?" Oliver affectionately rumpled Sally's hair, then showed her the kitchen. The effect of his strong hand on her arm sparked sudden tears, and she swallowed the surge of grateful emotion in her throat.

Here in Evanville, this tiny diner and everyone in it had welcomed her, and she felt happier than she'd been in ages.

A few minutes later, she tugged her hair back with a ponytail holder, rolled up her sleeves, and faced him at the sink while they washed their hands.

"I can't wait to watch you doing what you do best." He handed her a clean apron. "I never imagined the most prominent candymaker in Bloomingfield would be in my diner."

As she tied the apron about her waist, she quipped, "Be prepared to taste the finest candy Evanville has ever experienced. But only if you promise to help me with cleanup afterward."

He chuckled. "It's a deal."

CHAPTER FOUR

$\mathcal{C}$ooking with Sally in his cozy diner proved strangely intimate, Oliver thought.

Hyper focused, Sally concentrated on melting and stirring chips and margarine, while Oliver spread thick chocolate into mini-muffin tins. He seldom spoke, allowing his cooking companion to work with no interruptions.

He attempted to concentrate, but in the comfortable ambiance of his kitchen, he was more absorbed in pondering the remarkable turn of fate that had caused Sally Elliot to wind up at his diner. For many reasons, beginning with his failed marriage, his first consideration was that it would have been better if Sally hadn't been stranded at his diner, because of his instant attraction to her.

However, after the last few hours establishing a friendship, she was compelling him to acknowledge and contemplate everything he'd missed since his divorce, and the fact that he'd hidden behind the familiar confines of his small-town diner.

A safe refuge. Not that there was anything wrong with that.

He gave himself a firm mental shake.

Nonetheless, he wanted to experience life again. And all this reflection had begun with a beautiful, vivacious, and intelligent woman who was busily creating candy across from him. She stopped in the process of stirring chocolate and raised her gaze to his, the color of her soft eyes reminding him of colorful blue cornflowers. Shiny, golden highlights around her face accentuated her ivory skin. Her lips were full, the perfect shade of pink.

"You're not spreading," she reminded.

"Sorry." He laughed. "By the way, do you want to sit down?"

"I'm okay." She hesitated, but remained doggedly standing. "Thank you for asking, though."

They exchanged cheerful nods and went quietly back to their tasks.

Deep in contemplation, he studied her.

What if she'd entered his diner two years ago, when his divorce was still raw? Would he have noticed her then, or would he have been wallowing in the hurt and disappointment, the mistrust of his once-wife leaving him for his best friend?

Would he have admired her high cheekbones and soft lips, her slim figure and gorgeous, thick hair?

He blew out a silent sigh. Yes, he concluded, he would have admired her charm, her straightforwardness, her work ethic. However, he wouldn't have taken the relationship any further.

Absently, he grinned at her offhand remark that if he chose to cook, he was also slated for cleanup duty. This woman drove a hard bargain.

She slanted him a teasing smile, gazing at him with those incredibly striking eyes. "Cat got your tongue, Mr. Oliver?"

He was so lost in his reflections, he jumped at her question.

"Some people like more chocolate, some less," he advised, waving his wooden spoon jokingly in the air.

"Shouldn't you use a measuring cup so that all the candy is even?"

He raised an eyebrow. "Nope."

"Well we're about out of semisweet chips." Sally plunked her hands on her hips. "What should we do with the leftover peanut butter mixture?"

"That's where your specialty chocolate comes in." He opened the box of bittersweet chocolate and spooned a modest amount into the semisweet chips. Deftly, he stirred, then heated the remainder.

"Innovation is the mother of—" he began.

"The saying is, 'Necessity is the mother of invention,'" she corrected, a smile flickering across her face. "However, you are an impressive innovator."

"A trait learned from my father. We were poor, so he learned to make do with what we had—simple, wholesome food. Although, observing and listening to you inspires me to want to pursue more formal chef training."

She beamed, the sort of beam that begins from within and cannot be contained. "You're an expert in your own right, Oliver."

She stood by his side while they continued to portion and bake. Continuously distracted by her, he admired the easy, natural way she handled herself in the kitchen—a pinch of this, a shake of that, then meticulously measuring the key ingredients. As he did his own mixing, he reminisced about his boyhood in Evanville and the happy-go-lucky days of his youth before his mother got sick, then his father, leaving him at an inexperienced age to raise a twelve-year-old sister.

Sally chatted about her daughter and touched on the piercing defeat of losing her husband when she'd needed him most, and Oliver's heart squeezed.

"Ben came to my rescue." Tears welled in her eyes, and she wiped them away with the back of her hand. "I'm sorry for getting so emotional."

"Please don't apologize," he said.

"All these years I've numbed my emotions and immersed myself in work."

"I completely understand," he commiserated. "Much the same happened to me." He was silent for a beat before setting down his spoon and tipping up her chin. "I imagine being a single mother isn't easy, but I bet you're the best mother in the world."

"Clarissa is my greatest reward." Sally's flawless complexion fairly glowed whenever she mentioned her daughter. Without hesitation, she continued, "Oliver, I was thinking."

"Forever dangerous where women are concerned." At her frown, he prodded, "Thinking about what?"

"When I leave here tonight, who will shower me with compliments?"

"Compliments will definitely be forthcoming." His heartbeat doubled as he shifted closer. For a moment, he debated. Should he kiss her? Was it too soon? They'd only met a few hours earlier.

He did kiss her, but opted for a sweet brush of his lips on her forehead.

"Hey, you two lovebirds! It's not Valentine's Day yet!" Emily burst into the kitchen with the others in tow. "How long does it take to make a few peanut butter cups?"

"The first batch is ready," Sally said.

Emily snatched one up. "Delicious," she declared, and the

newlyweds agreed as they shared bites. Joe grabbed two, stating that he deserved more than the others because he'd delivered the chocolate.

"Not quite all the way to my shop," Sally reminded him.

"Close enough," came his response.

"Too sweet," the older woman proclaimed, refusing to eat another bite.

"Not sweet enough," her husband declared, devouring an entire peanut butter cup and then seizing the rest of hers.

Oliver split a peanut butter cup with Sally. They stood closer together, his arm brushing against hers, the air between them fairly charged with an electrical current. He knew she recognized the change in their relationship from when she'd first scurried into the diner. He knew that as surely as he knew that he wanted to see her again, *planned* on seeing her again.

He wanted to appreciate the contagious ring of her laughter, their easy-going banter. He hoped to meet her adorable daughter.

And he wanted to feel her lips pressed against his.

*C*losing hour at the Bloomingfield Candy Shop couldn't arrive soon enough, Sally mused three days later. The last of the customers had picked up their orders, and there was scarcely a piece of candy left in the store.

Valentine's Day sales were a success.

Bone tired, she bent to arrange two red lollipops that had toppled over on the white display case. The chocolate coffee fudge had won out over her infusion salted caramel candies as the store's bestselling Valentine candy.

Her thoughts drifted to Olive's Diner, the night she'd been stranded.

Initially, she'd intended to bring home the peanut butter cups she'd prepared, but the candy hadn't made it out of the diner. The newlyweds, Emily, and Joe had waxed poetic about the flavor with every bite. The older couple, not so much.

She grinned. The wonderful people she'd met were the ideal antidote to her crazy work life. Since then, she decided she wanted other people's opinions of her products, that is, people who weren't in her business—her staff and candymakers.

She'd brought up the idea of monthly taste-testings to Ben, who, as she'd anticipated, had scolded her for taking on additional work. Nonetheless, she intended to go ahead with her new idea.

"*Spontaneous people have more fun*," Oliver had said.

Still, planning was important if a person wished to get things accomplished.

Oliver. She had to put him out of her mind, but even while she told herself that, her musings returned to the diner.

By the time the tree in the middle of the road had been cleared, she hadn't arrived home until after midnight, with a case full of specialty chocolate, minus one pound.

She gathered a deep breath. Oliver hadn't texted her since she left Evanville, although he'd requested her phone number. Perhaps she'd return to his diner with Clarissa and order the meat loaf and mashed potatoes that wasn't on his menu.

"*It's not on the menu because customers know I have it,*" he'd said.

Truly the man needed someone to advise him on how to run a profitable business. And if he didn't contact her by the end of the week, she'd contact him.

No, no, she couldn't do that, a desperate attempt at a relationship with a man who might not be interested. She'd done that once already, and her marriage to Leon had almost destroyed her self-esteem.

She paused, her thoughts circling back to Oliver, as they often did. In the midst of an impromptu candy-making session, she'd found something she'd searched for her entire life.

Contentment. Joy in a simple project.

And maybe, just maybe, a good, sincere man.

"*I*'m leaving," Ben said. "Congratulations on a remarkably successful holiday." He grabbed his jacket. "Maise and I are dining out tonight."

"Is it one of her food critic jobs?" Sally asked.

"No. Although she does it for work, she loves going out for pleasure. Please join us."

"I can't." Sally declined with an apologetic sigh. "I'm committed to mac and cheese with Clarissa."

"Valentine's Day is over."

"I know, but barely."

"We're going to Julie's restaurant, and you love her homemade fettuccini."

"Some other night. Soon. I promise."

"That's what you always say," he reminded.

As he walked out the door, Sally called after him, "We'll take a raincheck."

Five minutes later, as she was rearranging a display that had little candy left, the bell on the door jingled, indicating one more customer. She stifled a groan. Hadn't Ben posted the closed sign?

"Sally?" The deep male voice made her pause.

She hesitated for a second before she spun. Her heart beat double time, taking in his strong, athletic features, his wonderful smile. "Oliver?"

"Your hair looks ... different. Wonderful."

There was no mistaking the huskiness in his tone. She

couldn't free her stare from his intent gaze. "I used a hair straightener." She fingered a strand that had come loose from her ponytail. "Do you like it?"

"You look gorgeous, whether your hair is curly or straight." He strode to her, bearing a foil-covered plate. "I brought you something for Valentine's Day."

She stepped over to him, peering at the plate as he uncovered it. Peanut butter cups, unevenly spaced, some thicker than others.

"I've been trying these out for the past two days, incorporating some ideas you suggested about working with chocolate." He offered that boyish grin. "I'm not claiming these peanut butter cups are better than your fancy infusion candies, but . . ."

As he chatted, she plucked up a candy and took a bite. "Oliver, this is amazing." She closed her eyes, allowing the flavors of peanut butter and chocolate to melt on her tongue.

"I used more sugar."

"Excellent." She grinned. "Perhaps we can start selling your peanut butter cups in my shop."

"Are they as delicious as my vegetable soup?"

"I don't know. I never had the opportunity to try your soup."

"I'll make it again." He set the candy aside, took her in his arms and brushed a kiss on her mouth. "Just for you."

Just for her. His words swirled around in her mind. His voice lowered, his gaze loving, his lips tasting of chocolate.

She drew a quiet, steadying inhale, shaking her head at her resolutions to avoid love. With Oliver, there was no need for false pride and relationship games.

Because the truth was, in the short time she'd known him, she had begun to fall in love with him. And by his affectionate gaze, the romantic way he stroked her cheek, he felt the same about her.

"Happy Valentine's Day, Sally," he said. "And thank you."

She cleared her throat to prevent her voice from shaking. "Whatever for?"

"For coming into my diner. For looking beautiful and never missing a single step, no matter the obstacles. And for creating the most delectable candy in the world for me and my customers."

"Not as tasty as your diner food."

"Because diner food is the best." He laughed and linked his fingers through hers. "Miss Sally Elliot, about all that planning you do ..."

She tipped back her head, smiling at him with wide-eyed innocence. "Me?"

"I'm available if you can squeeze me into your calendar." His tone was firm. He wouldn't allow otherwise. "And I'd love to meet your daughter."

"How about tonight?"

His gaze searched hers, glinting with amusement. "You're being spontaneous?"

"Absolutely. I'm picking Clarissa up at the sitter's in a few minutes." Quickly, Sally adjusted her plans. "How would you like to go to dinner with us at my sister's restaurant?"

"The Pasta Junction?"

"Everyone will be there. Ben and Maise, and Lorenzo, the TV weatherman. He and Julie are dating."

"Count me in." His deep voice had a precarious effect on her heart beat. "Sounds like the perfect Valentine's Day celebration."

She eyed his handsome features, his poignant smile, the look in his eyes—warm and inviting. He was her Valentine. Now and always.

Because, she realized, it's your last love who truly matters.

he End

RECIPE FOR AMY'S PEANUT BUTTER CUPS

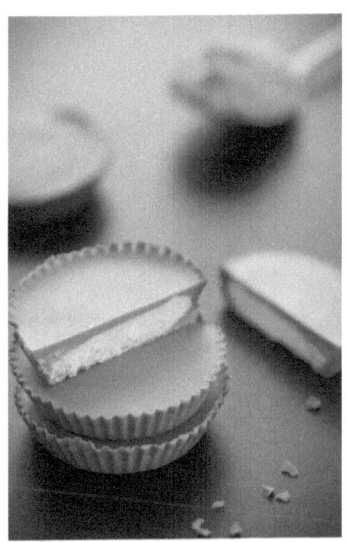

Bottom layer:

    2 sticks margarine melted

    1 18-ounce jar peanut butter

    2 sleeves graham crackers, crushed

    1 pound powdered sugar

Mix until well blended

Top layer

1 12-ounce bag semisweet chocolate chips

1 stick margarine

Melt together in the microwave for about 90 seconds, stirring halfway through.

Place bottom layer in the prepared tins and pour the top layer over it.

Prepare in mini muffin or regular sized tins. The thickness of the chocolate can be varied according to your preferences.

Can also be done in a 9x13 dish and cut into squares.

A NOTE FROM JOSIE

Dear Friends,

Thank you for reading *A Chocolate-Box Valentine*.

This is a short story for a quick, sweet read.

I wanted to write a Valentine romance centering around chocolate, which continues the story of my other *Chocolate-Box* books.

If you loved this romance as much as I loved writing it, please help other people find *A Chocolate-Box Valentine* by posting your review.

A Chocolate-Box Valentine is available in ebook, paperback, Large Print paperback, and Audiobook.

I'd love to meet you in person someday, but in the meantime, all I can offer is a sincere and grateful thank you. Without your support, my books would not be possible.

As I write my next sweet or inspirational romance, remember this: Have you ever tried something you were afraid to try because it mattered so much to you? I did, when

I started writing. Take the chance, and just do something you love.

My Spotify Play List for A Chocolate-Box Valentine is here.

With sincere appreciation,

Josie Riviera

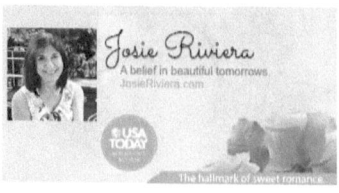

Love sweet romance Valentine stories?

Be sure to check out my other books:

I Love You More

A Valentine To Cherish

1-800-CUPID

Valentine Hearts: A 3 book Valentine Bundle

Want more of the Chocolate-Box Series?

Click here.

And be sure to read: A Chocolate-Box Summer Breeze

ACKNOWLEDGMENTS

An appreciative thank you to my patient husband, Dave, and our three wonderful children.

ABOUT THE AUTHOR

Josie Riviera is a *USA TODAY* bestselling author of contemporary, inspirational, and historical sweet romances that read like Hallmark movies. She lives in the Charlotte, NC, area with her wonderfully supportive husband. They share their home with an adorable shih tzu, who constantly needs grooming, and live in an old house forever needing renovations.

To receive my Newsletter and your free sweet romance novella ebook as a thank you gift, sign up HERE.

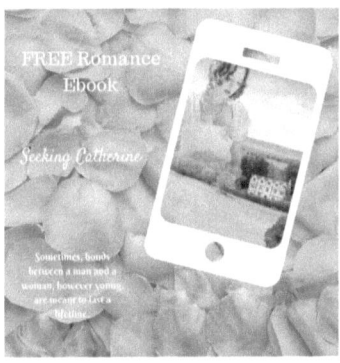

Become a member of my
 Read and Review VIP Facebook
 group for exclusive giveaways and FREE ARC's.

josieriviera.com/

josieriviera@aol.com

ALSO BY JOSIE RIVIERA

Cherished Hearts Six Book Volume

Aloha To Love

Sweet Peppermint Kisses

Valentine Hearts Boxed Set

1-800-CUPID

1-800-CHRISTMAS

1-800-IRELAND

1-800-SUMMER

1-800-NEW YEAR

The 1-800-Series Sweet Contemporary Romance Bundle

Irish Hearts Sweet Romance Bundle

Holly's Gift

A Chocolate-Box Christmas

A Chocolate-Box New Years

A Chocolate-Box Valentine

A Chocolate-Box Summer Breeze

A Chocolate-Box Christmas Wish

A Chocolate-Box Irish Wedding

Chocolate-Box Hearts

Chocolate-Box Hearts Volume Two

Chocolate-Box Double Hearts

Recipes From The Heart

Leading Hearts

New Year Hearts

SENIOR HEARTS

Summer Hearts

Christmas in the Air (1-800-Book)

A Very Christian Christmas

Most books are available in ebook, audiobook, paperback, Large Print paperback and Hardcover.

Many are FREE on Kindle Unlimited!